THREE MILITARY SF NOVELLAS

KEVIN J. ANDERSON

WFP
WORDFIRE PRESS

Three Military SF Novellas
by Kevin J. Anderson

Ebook ISBN: **978-1-61475-990-4**
Trade Paperback ISBN: **978-1-61475-989-8**
Hardcover ISBN: **978-1-61475-991-1**
Cover design by Janet McDonald
Cover artwork images by Adobe Stock
Kevin J. Anderson, Art Director

Published by
WordFire Press, LLC
PO Box 1840
Monument CO 80132
Kevin J. Anderson & Rebecca Moesta, Publishers
Printed in the USA

Join our WordFire Press Readers Group for free books,
sneak previews, updates on new projects, and other giveaways
Sign up at wordfirepress.com

CONTENTS

COMRADES IN ARMS

1

Palming the power stud on his laser rifle, Rader leaped into the alien trench and sighted on his enemy. Targeting vectors appeared on the inner surface of his helmet face shield, and the tactile sensors on his gloves linked to his artificial hands.

Ten Jaxxans skittered along the angled trenches they had dug as they made progress across the planetoid's contested landscape. Moving in ranks, they all reacted in unison to his arrival. The enemy did not like, did not *understand*, unpredictability.

As a Deathguard, Rader was unpredictable. He had been designed that way.

He found his balance on the loose pea-gravel, used his momentum to keep charging forward. In their open bug-tunnels, the Jaxxans had no room to scatter, nor did they have time.

The brain fire pounded through him, the Werewolf Trigger

that insisted he kill, *KILL!* He was a well-armored bull-in-a-china-shop, brain still alive along with a patchwork of his original body, hooked up to spare parts that allowed him to be sent back onto the battlefield. The chaos he provoked was part of a tactical plan issued by officers far from the battlefield; Death-guards weren't expected to survive long, though.

Rader had been briefed about this as a new recruit, though he hadn't ever considered it a real possibility while he and his squadmates laughed about squashing roaches. But the officials had made him the offer, showing him the contract as he lay there hooked up to complex life-support mechanisms in the med-center bed. Rader had barely been able to read the type with his one remaining eye.

"You want this, soldier? Or would you rather just be disconnected?"

The answer had seemed obvious. At the time.

Now the first alien died before he even saw the Death-guard: a pinpoint of red laser light burned through his chitinous face. Cyborg components kicked in, and Rader swiveled, sweeping the area with the nose of his weapon. Energy gels and synthetic adrenaline kept him moving, kept him shooting.

There were ten Jaxxans, then seven, then four in the invisible wake of his beam.

Much of the surface of the planetoid Fixion was a no-man's land, slashed with enemy trenches and tunnels interspersed with watchtowers. The aliens liked geometric order, but used unsettling angles, tilted planes, rarely straight lines. They had already occupied twenty asteroids in the Fixion Belt, just as the human army had; now both sides fought over the rest of the territory, particularly this central planetoid.

No longer part of the Earth League forward lines, Rader had already served his term as a soldier, given it his all, and now had this "opportunity" to give some more, for as long as he might last. He was there as an independent berserker, armed and juiced, sent into the no-man's land without any obvious military objective—it drove the Jaxxans nuts.

Deathguards were expensive and effective, categorized as Vital Equipment rather than Personnel—and so far the PR victories had been worth every penny of the military's investment. Or so Rader had heard; he was not on the list for explanations.

In short order, he killed eight of the Jaxxans in the trench, but he found himself wound in the luminous green threads of an energy-web cast by the last two aliens. The mentally projected web closed around him in a glowing net that would short out his armor and destroy his components—both the artificial ones and his biological ones.

But the Werewolf Trigger screamed at him like a drill sergeant inside his head. KILL! KILL! And he obeyed. The last of the Jaxxans fell to the trench floor, angular limbs twitching, and the coalescing energy-web faded.

The mindless Werewolf Trigger died to a whisper as the threat diminished and he calmed himself. Now that Rader could see more than a red haze, he gazed upon the carnage. The filters in his helmet blocked out the stench of burned meat and boiled ichor.

Alone, Rader recorded high-res images of the dead enemy in the trenches, transmitted his kills to HQ, and received acknowledgment but no praise.

He didn't need to remind himself that these Jaxxans

weren't *human*. He stared at their scattered bodies, trying to compare them to something from Earth; they evoked locusts, lizards, and skeletons all at once. The aliens were unnaturally thin, with tough skin that resembled chitin. Their eyes were striking, large black globes that reflected the goldenrod light of Fixion's sun.

The Jaxxans carried no weapons, nor did they encase themselves in armor. All their power, their energy-webs, and everything else about them (he wasn't sure how much was rumor and how much was truth) originated in the minds behind those eerie polished eyes. Many Jaxxans supposedly studied human culture and language, but he hadn't had a chance for conversation to confirm it.

The walls of the shallow trench rolled inward, sliding down to cover the bodies. The sandy, gravelly soil of Fixion was lousy for digging trenches in—not to mention lousy for growing things in, lousy for building things in, lousy for living in. As a matter of honor, the Earth League would never let the Jaxxans have it, and the alien command apparently felt the same way.

Time to move on, keep finding targets, keep causing trouble—Commissioner Sobel had told him he might have four weeks of operational capability before the brain/cyborg interface deteriorated. He followed the Jaxxan trench, taking the path of least resistance, but he encountered no other Jaxxans. The trench bent in one direction, then another, but ultimately went nowhere.

Off in the distance, near the asteroid's foreshortened horizon, human artillery brought down a tall Jaxxan watchtower, and soldiers clashed in a forward offensive as part of the official military plan. His comrades. *Former* comrades.

Rader didn't belong there, would not be going back to the main base on the far side of Fixion, would not be going home.

He climbed out of the trench and set off across the open landscape.

2

————

On the very last day that Rader (Rader, Robert: 0166218: Earth-Boston) lived as a grunt, he rode inside a spearhead-shaped assault fighter, enthusiastic about the impending engagement. He crowded next to his buddies on the hard metal benches, hunched over, counting down the seconds until they reached the Jaxxan nesting asteroid.

They were a team, comrades in arms. No time for second thoughts now.

The cold metal air had been recycled too many times but still carried the unmistakable odors of sweat and farts, obvious indicators of human tension. Rader was pumped up on metabolic supplements and foul-tasting power goo. At the Base, he had wolfed down a chewy high-protein breakfast cake, which was supposed to taste like bacon and eggs, before rushing to the assault ship, grabbing his weapon, securing his body armor, and getting mentally prepared.

His squad mates were ready to go squash some roaches. They had been cooped up far too long at the Earth League's Fixion Base #1, participating in simulation after simulation, blowing up fearsome holographic Jaxxans during practice sessions.

So far, Rader had been on only one real assault mission, a raid on a Jaxxan supply ship. Hundreds of Earth League forces had captured the small alien craft, and they had slaughtered every enemy aboard without any difficulty; Rader barely got off a shot. In battle simulations, the holographic alien warriors had always fought much more fiercely. He suspected that the Jaxxans on the supply ship were just civilians hauling crates of packaged food.

Today's assault was bound to be much more challenging.

The night before, while prepping for the mission, Squad Sergeant Blunt had given them the full briefing—and "blunt" he was indeed, although the word "gruff" seemed equally appropriate; some of Rader's squad mates preferred the term "psycho-bastard." Rader had sat joking with his buddies, nudging ribs with elbows. Since being thrown together into the same pressure cooker with the same goal and the same enemy, their squad had become very close—Renfrew, Chaney, Coleman, Rajid, Gonzalez, Huff.

In the briefing room, Sergeant Blunt projected a map of the asteroid belt, a smattering of space gravel strewn along an orbit that just happened to be in the star's habitable zone, though no one would really want to live there. Nevertheless, the Earth League deemed the Fixion Belt worth fighting for, and Rader had signed up in a fit of patriotism that had lasted significantly less time than his term of service.

The Sarge pointed to illuminated asteroids on the diagram, indicating the ones held by humans and an equivalent number held by Jaxxans. (The score received boos and hisses from the squad members). The largest planetoid, Fixion itself, was the most hotly fought-over piece of real estate in the Galaxy.

Blunt pointed to another flyspeck amid the dots in the asteroid belt. "Intel has discovered a roach hatching base, or a nest, or whatever the hell they call it. We're going to wipe it out. Squash the bugs before they can hatch a thousand more disgusting soldiers."

The Sarge paused for a moment, looking at every member of the squad. "Payback. The Roaches did the same thing to us on Cephei Outpost. They saw that little colony and assumed it was our breeding station, killed all those poor colonists, those children. I don't think they understand how humans breed." Sergeant Blunt's voice became grim and angry. "We've got embassies set up on the Détente Asteroid, and the Jaxxan higher-ups speak better English than you do, but neither side talks."

The mood in the briefing room grew resentful; many of the grunts sneered at the very idea of peace talks. Huff let out a rude snort. "How can you talk with the *things* that slagged Cephei?"

Sergeant Blunt got them to concentrate on the priority. "It's not your job to think about the big picture. We don't pay you enough to consider the complicated things. Commissioner Sobel decides when it's time to talk to them. For you guys, we keep it simple: Enter the roach hatching station, destroy everything, and go home."

Rader raised his hand. "Any intel on Jaxxan defenses there, Sergeant?"

"Doesn't matter." The Sarge gave the closest thing to a smile that Rader had ever seen. "We'll have a Deathguard with us. A fresh one, all systems still fully functional."

A quick hesitation of surprise, then a round of cheers ...

Later, as the assault fighter closed in on the targeted Jaxxan hatching base, Rader checked his weapon, his suit, his med kit, his backup power pack. He pretended to relax. Waiting ... gearing up ... waiting ... joking ... waiting. Typical Earth League operation: hurry up and wait.

Voices grew louder in the spacecraft as the conversation became edgier, more rushed. He and his buddies talked about what they would do on their next R&R, reminisced about their homes, their families, their sweethearts. Although his squadmates were not a particularly handsome lot, each man claimed to have a gorgeous girlfriend who put porn holostars to shame and yet was entirely loyal and head-over-heels in love.

After the massacre on Cephei Outpost, he'd been too young by a month when the first call went out. But his best friend, Cody, was two months older and just barely squeaked into the Earth League military, ready to go after the Jaxxans. Before he left for basic training, Cody said goodbye to Rader with a quick embrace and then a studiously practiced League handshake. "There'll be plenty of roaches for both of us to kill, don't worry! Get your ass in the League as soon as you can sign up, and I'll meet you out there." He gestured vaguely toward the sky. Rader promised, waving ... but wishing his friend had waited, just a couple of months.

His parents and his sister worried about Rader going off to war, but it was the patriotic thing to do. All healthy young men were pressured to join up, and he was anxious to follow in Cody's footsteps. A month later, on his birthday, he filled out the forms.

One week into basic training at the lunar military base, Rader received word that Cody and his entire squad had been wiped out by an equipment malfunction. An airlock hatch blew open when the troop transport was approaching a space station. Explosive decompression killed all personnel, sucked them out into space. Simple mechanical failure, bad luck—nothing that could be blamed on the enemy.

Rader had joined wanting to fight alongside Cody. They had always been a team, and he had hoped they could support each other, stand together against the Jaxxans. But the Earth League had him now, and he couldn't change his mind. His squadmates were his comrades now, his new best friends....

As soon as the assault shuttle landed on the Jaxxan nesting asteroid, explosive bolts would blast the hatch open so that the soldiers could storm out in a howling rush. His companions whooped, winding themselves up during the final approach, and Rader joined in. But as he looked warily at the hatch, suited up and holding his laser rifle, he thought of Cody's last moments ... willing to die in a blaze of glory out on the battle-field, not from a stupid malfunction.

Sitting wordless on an empty bench, the Deathguard in their team was an ominous, armored form, like a knight in shining armor. Rader respected the powerful cyborgs—resuscitated, revamped, and restructured to become perfect fighting machines—though he wondered what thoughts kept them going. Did they focus on the mission, even knowing what had happened to them, and what *would* happen to them? He supposed it was better than being declared dead. All Deathguards got an honorable funeral, and their families received full pensions; no one knew the former identity of any individual Deathguard. Rader hadn't thought twice about it when he enlisted in the League. He'd signed up body and soul.

Huff leaned over and whispered to him, "I can't wait to see that Deathguard go bonkers on the roach nest."

"So long as he doesn't go all Werewolf on us before it's time," Rajid said.

Rader found himself staring at the silent cyborg. "Not going to happen. They're too sophisticated for that." The Deathguard made no comment, one way or another.

Through the small windowport on his side of the craft, Rader could see the potato-shaped asteroid as they closed in. The large craters were covered over with domes like large blisters, as if the space rock had reacted with an outbreak of boils to the alien presence.

Sergeant Blunt walked in heavy boots from the front bulkhead and stood before them in full uniform armor. "Listen up. Based on the small number of roach military ships stationed at the asteroid, looks like the enemy has no major defenses here. We have no intel on the interior of the base, so you'll have to find your way. Get to the main hatching chamber and destroy it. Clear enough? Your job is simple—point and shoot."

On the way in, the assault ship's pulsed lasers disabled the four Jaxxan ships stationed at the nest asteroid. Even though the nest asteroid sent emergency calls for Jaxxan reinforcements, Sergeant Blunt had expected it. The plan was to strike fast and finish the operation before alien backup vessels could fly in.

"All right, children," the Sarge said. "Saddle up, take your toys, and let's go scramble some eggs. Just don't let them scramble you. We're coming in hot, going to blow through one of their entrance domes. Do I need to remind you that this is *not* a prisoner capturing mission?"

"No, Sarge!" they all chimed in.

"Good, I was hoping you weren't all as dense as you looked. Now let's move it." The Sergeant fitted a breathing mask over his face; Rader and his companions did the same. The Deathguard sat waiting, like a missile prepped for launch.

Once the assault shuttle careened up against the largest blister dome and a shaped-charge explosion blasted open the hatch to let them loose, Rader's squadmates boiled out, swinging their laser rifles and yelling; they exercised just enough restraint to keep from shooting one another.

The alarms inside the hatching base sounded like staccato clacking beetles. Rader bolted forward and used his laser rifle to cut down any aliens he encountered. It wasn't his place to decide whether the roaches were civilians, politicians, medical personnel, or soldiers.

In the back of his mind, he wondered if the Jaxxan assault squad on Cephei Outpost had operated under similar orders.

As they rounded a corner into the main base, a Jaxxan in front of them raised his thin forearms and wove a deadly psychic energy-web. Gonzalez let out a cry more of surprise than pain, then the incandescent green lines disintegrated him.

Astonished, Rader used the sudden jolt of shock and fired.

He blasted the Jaxxan before he could move his angular arms again.

Behind the main squad, the Deathguard lurched into the fray, mowing down targets, yet never coming close to hitting one of his human comrades. The cyborg blew open door hatches, thrust his armored body into well-lit research chambers, annihilated any aliens he found working in their labs. Then the Deathguard pushed forward, leading the way along skewed corridors and through angled intersections, deeper into the hatching base.

Still off-balance and angry from the loss of Gonzalez, Rader ran headlong with four of his comrades into a chamber of horrors—a nursery. Five Jaxxan attendants had lined up to protect more than a dozen fat, squirming grubs, white segmented things like maggots the size of alligators.

Coleman said, "That's just *wrong!*" He opened fire, and the grubs spilled open like fleshy sacs filled with entrails and ichor.

Frantic, one of the Jaxxan caretakers cried out in English, "No! Not the offspring." The alien's comprehensible words were so startling that Rader hesitated. But it was just a ruse: other aliens nearby worked together to weave a sparkling energy-web, filling the air with a mesh of green that they cast toward the human soldiers.

Rader focused and shot one of the roaches, then the next, working his way down the line, just like in the simulation. Huff knocked out the other two, and their incomplete energy-web dispersed. The rest of the Earth League soldiers made swift work of the remaining grubs in the nursery, chopping them into chunks of meat.

The Deathguard, who wasn't part of the formal operation,

had already moved ahead on his own, continuing his rampage. Apparently, the cyborg soldier wanted to make the most of his second chance.

Over the implanted radio, Rader heard Sergeant Blunt yelling from a different sector of the asteroid, "Just woke up a hundred roach warriors in the deep tunnels! And they look angry. Called Base for reinforcements. Another ship should be here in an hour or two, so hold the roaches off till then."

"Roger that, Sarge," came a chorus of responses.

The Sarge added, "We know they sent off a distress signal too. It'll be a race to see who gets here first."

Rader said with genuine bravado, "Won't leave anything for them to rescue, Sarge."

As the squad pushed into the asteroid's most secure chambers, desperate Jaxxans fought harder and harder. Energy-webs rippled down the angled corridors, ricocheting off stone walls and frying several more human soldiers. Rader kept a rough score in the back of his mind, tried not to name his friends who lay dead. *Concentrate on the operation, on the objective.*

So far, he thought the humans were taking a greater toll.

Explosions rippled through the nesting base, and over-pressure waves made his ears pop. Sergeant Blunt shouted over the implanted radio, "Heavy resistance—fresh warriors from below." He paused, as if to listen to a report. "Ah, crap— there's a roach ship coming in! Don't know if we can hold 'em off long enough." Rader heard another explosion, a sizzling sound, then a cry of pain from the Sarge—a high-pitched yelp that did not at all sound like the gruff, hardboiled man—then only static on the comline.

Rader shoved aside his alarm and dismay, not sure how the

survivors of his squad were going to get out of here, but they would keep pushing toward the objective.

He, Coleman, and Huff fought their way into a large guarded chamber where the roaches made their last stand. The entrance hatch was sealed, so the three soldiers used their laser rifles to melt an entrance through the putty-like polymer metal wall.

"This must be the place," Coleman said.

Inside the protected chamber, Rader and his comrades discovered row after row of polished black casings the size of coffins.

"Giant eggs," Huff said. "Look at all of them!"

The soldiers opened fire on the casings, cracking them open and spilling out white and slippery humanoid forms with backward-jointed arms and legs, ovoid heads, and giant black eyes that were covered with a milky caul.

So they were chrysalises, not eggs.

With a high-pitched chitter, three Jaxxans lunged out from between the rows of black casings. When they hurled half-formed energy-webs, Rader dove out of the way, but Coleman was too busy shooting the chrysalises. The energy-web snared him, killed him.

Huff began firing wildly at the Jaxxans. From their cover, the aliens formed another energy-web that shimmered in the air and came toward them. Rader dropped to the floor and took cover, rolling up against one of the tall black casings. He yelled a warning, but Huff kept firing even as the web encircled and disintegrated him.

From his position of dubious shelter, Rader shot the two Jaxxans, then waited, listening.

Moving in a scramble of excessively jointed arms and legs,

another alien skittered forward to a split chrysalis and caught the albino, mostly formed creature as it slumped out of the cracked shell. Like a soldier holding a wounded comrade, the roach cradled the dying, half-formed creature in segmented arms.

Rader rose to his feet, and the Jaxxan swiveled its head toward him, showing those large, black eyes like pools of sorrow. "Look what you have done!" Though the creature's chitinous faceplates showed no emotions, Rader felt that the Jaxxan was giving him an accusatory glare.

A red spot appeared on the Jaxxan's forehead, and a laser blast cooked his encased head, exploding his entire skull.

The Deathguard strode into the chrysalis chamber. From behind the helmet, which was no more readable than the alien's face, the Deathguard looked at Rader, then turned back to the black cases. He began shooting them one by one.

Rader's implanted radio burst to life again. "This is Lieutenant Nolan with the reinforcement ship, closing in on the nesting asteroid. Two roach defenders got here before us. The asteroid's overrun, but we'll take 'em on! We don't leave men behind."

Rader didn't cheer the speech. He and the Deathguard were trapped in the chrysalis chamber. In the corridors outside, he could hear the ominous sound of hundreds of skittering legs—warriors that had been hiding deep inside the asteroid, and were now closing in on the chrysalis chamber. Rader joined the Deathguard, standing together as they shot the rest of the casings, knowing they didn't have much time ... knowing they weren't likely to get out alive.

At least he had a chance for some payback for his lost

comrades. It was the only thread of hope he had to cling to. He wished he and Cody could have been here together doing this.

The armored and silent Deathguard turned around and opened fire on the Jaxxan warriors that surged into the chamber. Sergeant Blunt had counted more than a hundred of them; to Rader, it seemed like a thousand. Lieutenant Nolan's reinforcements would never get here in time. The radio channel remained silent, no transmissions from the rest of his squadmates.

Backing deeper into the chrysalis chamber, the Deathguard worked his way in among the black casings. Rader thought their position by the door was more defensible, but then he realized that the Deathguard was making a calculated move to lure the roaches inside.

The Deathguard turned his unreadable helmet toward Rader again, expecting him to understand. From his armored casing, he removed a thermal-impulse grenade.

Rader's heart froze. The cyborg had nothing to lose. Rader could have made the same calculation as the Deathguard, but he was unwilling to come to the obvious conclusion. Nevertheless, the Deathguard was going to do it.

When all of the roach warriors charged into the chrysalis chamber and tried to corner the two remaining humans, the Deathguard lifted his grenade and depressed the activation button.

Rader dove among the cocoon casings in an instinctive, but futile gesture. The flash of dazzling white light was the last thing he ever expected to see.

BUT IT WASN'T.

The quality of light that came into focus had a harsh, sterile quality, and the surrounding brightness resolved itself into clean ceramic-plate walls—the Base's medical center. He could hear diagnostic scanners, medical machinery, a respirator breathing for him like a gasping schoolgirl. He felt no pain ... he felt nothing at all.

Rader couldn't move his head, only his eyes—one eye, actually—which limited his field of view. He tried to move, but could barely twitch his head ... in fact, he could feel nothing but his head. The rest of his body remained numb. Maybe he'd been paralyzed. Maybe he'd lost limbs. Maybe he'd lost everything.

A worried-looking orderly appeared in his field of view, staring down with brown, clinical eyes. Even in his condition, he didn't consider her pretty. "You're awake, aren't you?" she said. "Don't try to move. You're not ready for that yet. We haven't connected all the necessary pieces, still waiting for one part to be modified." She fiddled with one of the tubes hanging at his side. "There. Give it a few seconds."

Tranquilizers flooded into him, and he dropped back out of consciousness.

When Rader awoke again, a smiling man stood over him, a face that looked oddly familiar—not from personal experience, but from images on the news broadcasts. "Congratulations, soldier!"

Rader placed him as Commissioner Sobel, the man in charge of the Earth League forces in the Fixion Belt.

"The rest of your squadmates gave their lives to destroy the Jaxxan nesting asteroid. You fought bravely and kept yourself alive ... just barely, but it was enough. Your mission isn't over—not yet."

Rader tried to talk, but only croaking noises came out. He still had tubes in his throat.

Commissioner Sobel continued, "I'm congratulating you, soldier, because you have a second chance. A chance to join an elite group. Every one of your comrades gave their lives in service to the war, but you have an opportunity to keep fighting. Don't you want to hurt the enemy that did this to you?" He smiled. "We're offering you a position as our newest Deathguard."

Propped in the med-center bed, paralyzed in place, Rader couldn't see how much damage he had suffered from the explosion ... how much of *him* actually remained. Once they hooked him up to the cyborg components and encased him in his permanent armor, he doubted he would ever know.

Did it really matter?

A little extra time to carry on the fight. At the moment, he didn't quite see why that should be his priority; he would rather go home, say his farewells to his family, see Earth one more time. That second chance seemed more important.

"You're a hero and will be remembered as such, soldier. We're declaring the mission a success, now that we've looked at the cost-benefit ratio in detail. We did lose your Sergeant and your entire squad, but we successfully wiped out the Jaxxan nesting base. And you can honor them by replacing the Deathguard who died in the operation."

Rader was trying to speak, but no words came out. Sobel patted him on the shoulder—so, at least he *had* a shoulder. "We'll hook up your vocal cords in time for the official announcement, and then we'll turn you loose as a one-man army on the main Fixion battlefield. That's where you'll be most useful. Singlehandedly, you can create a hell of a lot of trouble. You'll have weeks, maybe even months before the interface breaks down. Cherish every moment of it—I know you'll accomplish as much as you can. We're all proud of you."

Sobel smiled again and then left. Rader hadn't been able to say a word.

3

Commissioner Sobel scowled at the insignia on his collar, still shiny from his recent transfer here. He was a dark-haired man, thirty pounds past good-looking: the kind whose face turned red very easily, and lately his face was turning red more than usual. He brushed off a few specks of dust and leaned back in the seat of his shuttle taking him from the Base to the Détente Asteroid. After six months, the useless embassy there was just beginning to feel familiar, though he doubted he would ever get used to Fixion.

As Commissioner, he was not foolish enough to believe the optimistic projections he sent back to Earth through the Information Bureau, but he had to make others believe them. Each report submitted for public dissemination had to show the human soldiers as faultless heroes and paint the Jaxxans as monstrous and alien. Fortunately, the Jaxxans looked hideous, and people had been programmed for centuries to fear bug-eyed monsters. How else could the Earth League maintain support for this abysmal war in this godforsaken place?

Humanity had a long history of shedding blood over worthless scraps of land, and this broken asteroid belt was one such place. Humans had visited there, established a tiny astronomical observatory, set up small outposts, planted their flags. So had the Jaxxans. When both governments dug in their heels, possessing Fixion and its entourage of habitable worldlets became a matter of honor.

Sobel was savvy enough to know that this war was not as senseless as it seemed. Rather, the Earth League—and no doubt the Jaxxans as well—used it as a practice field to test the mettle of the rival species and determine whether they wanted to prosecute a larger war across numerous star systems.

Three years ago, the aliens had showed their aggression (or maybe it had been a retaliation for something) by wiping out Cephei Outpost. So humans responded by blowing up any Jaxxan outpost they could find, and the two militaries began their nose-to-nose warfare on the main planetoid.

The people back home rallied, and recruiting offices had lines out the door. As the battles went on, the Deathguard cyborg killing machines were portrayed as warriors so tough that even death on the battlefield could not stop them from continuing the fight against the Jaxxans. Poignant, tragic, glorious.

Sobel's two predecessors had put in their time, and now he was stuck administering the Earth League forces. He ran the show out here, organized the military, sent back the PR dispatches.

For appearances sake, he was also the designated spokesman, an ambassador for humanity, charged (on paper at least) with finding a peaceful solution to the conflict. His superiors had never indicated that they genuinely desired a resolution; nevertheless, he needed to maintain appearances —he was good at that.

One of the small drifting rocks with a tenuous but stable atmosphere was named the Détente Asteroid, complete with a human embassy building and an adjacent Jaxxan embassy. By mutual agreement, each side was required to have a representative available at the embassy a certain percentage of the time, but due to a loophole in the agreement—intentional, Sobel thought—the human ambassador and the Jaxxan ambassador were not required to be on the Détente Asteroid *at the same time*, which made substantive peace talks difficult.

After a two-hour flight, Commissioner Sobel's shuttle landed on the Détente Asteroid. He was preoccupied enough with his thoughts that he forgot the oxygen mask until the last moment and fumbled it into place just as the hatch slid open.

He gathered his briefcase full of files, and followed a small honor guard across the landing zone to the embassy building; a vanguard entourage had already restored the power, heat, and air-generators. No one had occupied the building for weeks.

Not surprisingly, the corresponding Jaxxan embassy building was shut down: windows shuttered, doors locked, no one inside.

Sobel made quick work of settling in. Though it seemed a pointless obligation to be here, he did look forward to a few quiet and uninterrupted days. He had paperwork to review, forms to finish, consolation letters to write.

No matter what the Earth public saw in the glorious video footage sent by the Information Bureau—how human forces had pushed forward to gain a few more acres of the no-man's land, how the Deathguards continued to attack the enemy like heroic vigilantes—Sobel knew the war was not going well.

Something had to change soon. An unqualified victory would bring a surge in support on Earth, but even a devastating defeat would inflame their passions, and he could take advantage of that as well. The worst case was that the battle for the Fixion Belt was a stalemate that would continue for a long, expensive time. Since he and his Jaxxan counterpart, Warlord Kiltik, had no particular reason to hold meetings, no resolution was in sight.

Seated at his temporary desk, Sobel opened his briefcase. Before delving into the files he needed to review, he glanced through the tinted window at the closed Jaxxan embassy. As soon as the Commissioner left, Kiltik would arrive to serve his own time as mandated by the interim treaties, and he would go through the same motions.

4

Fixion's amber sky was barren of clouds, always. Even during the day, the tiny lights of other asteroids in the Belt were strung like a necklace overhead.

Dark spots speckled Rader's sandy brown armor, some camouflage, some just stains. Leaving the Jaxxan squad he had just killed, the Deathguard dodged across the landscape. Cover was easy to find on the torn-up terrain of canyons, craters, and angled trenches.

He noticed fighting in the distance and chose to head toward a collapsed Jaxxan watchtower. The Earth League operation had moved on, but if the roaches returned to begin repairs, maybe he could charge in among them. The Werewolf Trigger remained quiescent, but he didn't need it.

So far, all of his components functioned well. His brain moved the replacement parts in tandem with what remained of his body, but the breakdown could come at any time: a failed neural interface, a mechanical fault in the cyborg parts, or a collapse of life-support maintenance. The Earth League had drilled the duty into him: his commanding officers and comrades expected him to do everything in his power to defeat the Jaxxans.

He had accepted the terms in the med center: the extent of his injuries already categorized him as terminal, and he could either become a cyborg or be disconnected. In exchange for his new superhuman abilities he pledged to take on a solo mission that would not end until his final breath. His friend Cody had had no such opportunity.

Rader pushed on, alone, for as long as he might have left.

He dodged from one huge boulder to another, closing the distance to the damaged watchtower. He climbed an outcropping of rock above a steep gully, a crack in the shattered landscape from an ancient meteor impact. He stopped short, staring at the single Jaxxan that had taken cover in the gully below.

The alien was bent over a burnt human form—an Earth League soldier who had been charred by the backwash of an energy-web. Moving sharp-angled hands, the Jaxxan busily touched, inspected, prodded the soldier, who let out a groan of pain. The alien plucked a vial from a small open kit on the ground.

During basic training, Rader had heard of the awful things the roaches did to human bodies. He brought up his laser rifle and prepared to fire.

The alien looked at him with polished black eyes. He held a vial in long fingers, tilted it, and turned back to his work on the burned soldier.

With a jolt, Rader realized the open package on the ground

was a standard-issue Earth League med kit. The Jaxxan was *tending* the wounded man. The alien fumbled with the kit, swiveled his head back to Rader. "Assistance. Help me understand."

Roaches moved in groups, fought together, crowded in their trenches and hives; they were rarely encountered singly. This one would be easy prey. He kept the laser rifle pointed toward the alien, but did not fire.

The Jaxxan put a gauze pack down, inspected a different bottle. "How do I revive him?" He spoke in short, clipped syllables.

Confused, Rader slid down the side of the gully, still keeping his rifle ready. The injured man stirred, and Rader saw how horribly burned he was. He croaked with a voice he had rarely used since being turned loose as a Deathguard. "What are you doing?"

"No time." The alien chose a stim pack from the kit. "This one, I believe." He pressed it against the dying soldier.

Rader jabbed the laser rifle forward. "Stop!"

The alien continued his quick and efficient movements, either not intimidated by the Deathguard, or driven by other priorities. "I need to wake him before he dies." Although the Jaxxan's hard lips did not allow him to pronounce certain sounds correctly, Rader couldn't believe how well the Jaxxan spoke English.

His response should have been clear; he wasn't supposed to wonder. Why hadn't he killed the Jaxxan on first sight? Why hadn't the enemy tried to kill him?

And why was the alien trying so hard to revive a dying soldier?

The soldier's uniform identified him as a recon scout, a member of a small team sent to assess the aftermath of the earlier military operation. A moan escaped the man's blackened lips, and his eyes flickered open in terror and pain for an instant before he finally died.

The Jaxxan sat back on the ground, folding his long legs. He made a satisfied sound, then raised his face to the Deathguard. "Now you will kill me?"

Rader's eyes narrowed behind his darkened visor. "Why did you do that? Explain." He kept the laser rifle trained on the roach's chest.

The Jaxxan bowed his head, in what seemed to Rader an alien expression of guilt. *Anthropomorphizing.* Nothing more to it.

"My energy-web hit him from behind. I was afraid. He did not see me. He had no chance to know he was going to die." He paused as if waiting for Rader to understand. "His soul did not have time to prepare for the departure of death. Had he died without awakening, his soul would have remained trapped within the body, forever. I would not wish such a fate upon even my enemy."

Rader felt the hard rock against his armor as thoughts flashed through his mind. He also recalled the Jaxxan in the chrysalis chamber of the hatching asteroid, who had clung to the half-formed but dying alien as it slid out of the broken cocoon case. *Look what you have done.*

"How do you know our language?" He couldn't imagine any of his squadmates trying to learn to speak Jaxxan.

"I studied."

"Why?"

"Because you are interesting." Rader didn't know what to

say to that. "Many Jaxxans study humans. We review your broadcasts, your culture. I am a scholar, teacher, imaginer."

"Then what are you doing on the battlefield?"

"I was assigned to the System Holystal project. My interpretation of facets contradicted my superior's, and so I was transferred here."

Rader assessed the skeletal, buglike Jaxxan. He seemed scrawnier than most. "You don't look trained to be a soldier."

"Not trained. I was meant to die, in service." The alien studied him with eyes like molten pools of ink. "Why did you not kill me, Deathguard?"

Both remained silent for a long moment in a strange standoff. A shooting star sliced across the sky, bright enough to be seen against Fixion's amber daytime sky. "I don't know."

"You are confused, your emotions in turmoil. We are each supposed to kill the other, yet neither wants to."

Rader stiffened. He had not moved the laser rifle. "I may kill you yet."

"No. You will not."

"How can you be so sure?"

"I can read it in you." The Jaxxan cocked his head. "Did you not know we are empathic?"

"No." Command had neglected to include that detail in their briefings.

The Jaxxan shook his head in disappointment. "What is your name, Deathguard?"

The question itself opened old wounds. A name signified he was somebody, an individual. A hero killed in action during the raid on the nesting asteroid. That name, that person was dead; his family had the certificate to prove it, even though

Rader continued fighting for a brief period, like a mayfly in its final days.

"My name was Rader, before I was ... Now, I'm just a Deathguard." He sounded more gruff than he wanted to. He paused, wasn't sure why he even asked the question. "And your name?"

The Jaxxan proceeded to make a series of unpronounceable clicks from his alien gullet. Rader knew he could never repeat the name and said with a hint of humor. "I'd better just call you Click."

The alien seemed satisfied with that. "Rader, I must contemplate this turn of events. I was not prepared for such an occurrence. Please let me meditate." Still holding his laser rifle like a toy soldier positioned in place, the Deathguard regarded his enemy. Click answered the unspoken question. "I am not afraid of you. You will not harm me."

Rader was confused at such unwarranted trust, until he realized an empath could *feel* that Rader wasn't going to harm him. But how could he be so sure about Click? Maybe this was just a ruse to get him to drop his guard.

"You will want to bury your comrade." Click stood and moved away from the burned soldier. "That is the tradition."

Rader had just left the group of Jaxxans in the trench after killing them.

He could put the recon scout in a shallow grave, although Fixion had no known scavengers or predators that would disturb the body. He'd send a locator signal for an Earth League pickup crew to retrieve the fallen soldier. But, depending on where the fighting lines were, there was no telling when or if they would come. Due to interstellar shipping costs, bodies were never returned to Earth.

Yes, the recon scout deserved to be buried.

But Rader didn't know where he would go afterward. He had never let the question trouble him before. Days of running, fighting, killing tried to catch up with him, but internal mechanisms pumped stimulants into his body. He could rest here, but he could never sleep again—not after what they had done to him.

5

Since he already knew what Deathguards were, Rader figured out the implications even before the counselor came and rather impatiently explained his new situation. He'd had enough time in the med-center bed to draw his own conclusions.

"Your family has been notified of your heroic death, and the Earth League gave you a funeral with full military honors." He realized afterward that she did not use his name. "We sent home a clean packaged uniform, along with a posthumous medal of honor. The heirs designated on your enlistment form will receive a generous military combat pension."

His throat made noises, and he had to try several times before he could form the words. "Thank you."

She brushed the comment aside. She was rattling off a memorized speech and didn't want to be interrupted. "I regret to inform you that you are a terminal case. What remains of you belongs entirely to the Earth League. We will provide and maintain the machinery that keeps you alive." The counselor leaned closer to Rader. "We supply all of the equipment and components to make you whole again, temporarily. If you choose not to accept reconfiguration as a Deathguard, we will reclaim that equipment."

"Expiration ...?" He wanted to say much more, articulate a full sentence, but the counselor understood.

"How long will you last? Is that what you're asking? It varies. Each Deathguard is different, depending on the scope of injuries that put you here and the quality of the interface between your remains and our equipment." She looked down at a screen, touched a tab that activated his chart. "Not much left of you. I'm surprised you made it to the life-support bed on the rescue shuttle ... in fact, I'm amazed they bothered to carry the scraps there in the first place." Frowning, the counselor read further. "Ah. No other survivors from your squad. The Information Bureau must have needed to salvage something from the mission."

Rader didn't want to think about it, didn't want to recall his family either, or his friend Cody, or Earth. He wasn't supposed to have anything to look forward to. He was just an afterimage of his life.

"Look on the bright side, soldier. If you accept, you'll have years, or months, or weeks to keep up the fight—extra time that you wouldn't have had. When the Jaxxans try to understand our strategy and tactics, Deathguards are our ace in the hole, an element of random destruction they simply cannot predict." He had seen more convincing smiles on plastic mannequins. "You could well be the key to winning this war."

Rader had heard the pitch before, had even believed it when he went through basic training. He didn't argue. Judging by the counselor's flippant attitude, he imagined that she had little difficulty convincing other new Deathguards. He allowed them to put him back together again, Humpty-Dumpty in combat gear.

With the potential for malfunctions building day by day, the Base was anxious to get him tested and functional and back out onto the front lines. When they brought Rader up to speed on his defenses and prosthetics, he seemed to have one of everything he needed. The components functioned to design specs. He had his armor, his weapons, and his training.

Occasionally, during test exercises, he would catch glimpses of his skin, small patches that showed in between the armor plate. His flesh was so burned and scarred it looked like wadded, dried leather. He had no desire to see what he really looked like anymore.

He was trained to shoot automatically, accurately, and without remorse. A Werewolf Trigger had been implanted in his brain, activated by stress and perceived danger in a battle-field situation. And his self-preservation drive was dampened.

Without mentioning Rader's name, Commissioner Sobel introduced him with great fanfare in a cheery patriotic broad-cast sent out by the Information Bureau. "I give you the newest member of the Deathguard!" He raised Rader's gauntleted arm. Cheers resounded from the soldiers who had gathered at the Base for the formal announcement.

Despite the celebrations, Rader knew he could never be around people again. The Werewolf Trigger was like a firing pin in his brain, a siren that sounded off at oddball times. A Deathguard couldn't live back at the Base, nor bunk with other soldiers, not even fraternize with them. If something triggered his rampage, Rader could rack up countless casualties before he was terminated. From now on, he would be on his own.

The Commissioner's voice grew more somber. "Unfortunately, peace negotiations have broken down. Neither side is talking, and I don't expect the situation to improve. We'll need our Deathguards now more than ever."

More than a hundred of the deadliest, most powerful soldiers had been turned loose on the battlefield. Rader would join them, without comrades, in a last independent mission to create as much havoc as possible until his systems failed.

6

When he finished digging the grave and covering up the fallen recon scout, Rader looked across at Click. His cyborg senses and sensors had remained alert during the burial, but the Jaxxan hadn't moved.

The alien meditated peacefully, obsidian eyes staring off into nothingness. The air shimmered in front of his face to reveal a scintillating crystal that opened like a rosebud, a projected object half a meter across, glowing with prickly facets and spires—not a weapon like the energy-web, but a crystalline snowflake that hung by unseen threads. Click remained motionless, peering into the facets as if hypnotized.

Rader came closer, intrigued. This seemed delicate, wondrous.

Click spoke without looking up from his scrutiny. "This is my *holystal*: a holographic crystal that I create in my thoughts. A three-dimensional map of my life, what has happened and what may yet occur. Every possibility has its own facet, constantly shifting and re-emerging as circumstances change.

This ..." He reached out to touch a portion that was not symmetrical with the others. "This is where you fit in, Rader. Your presence has distorted all probable futures, giving me chances I should never have had, adding dangers that were not present before."

Rader was fascinated. "Can all Jaxxans do that? Or is it only you?"

Click made a rattling sound, and he realized the alien was laughing. "I am an imaginer, a scholar. My caste specializes in interpreting holystals, advising our leaders. Warlord Kiltik has his own expert on the System Holystal we are constructing in the Fixion Belt."

"And you disagreed with the expert, so you were punished."

"Yes. I was transferred to the battlefield." As Click spoke, the projected holystal shifted slightly, a gentle flickering of one facet into another. He pointed to the most prominent pinnacle. "This spire symbolizes that which is most important to me. It has stopped growing now. My work was my life, back in our home system ... before I was assigned here. To this war."

Rader thought of Cody, their own boyhood dreams, their plans for the future, but nothing so concrete as this crystalline blueprint of the Jaxxan's life.

Click continued with a distinct undertone of awe. "A team of engineers, scholars, imaginers, and dreamers was working on our race's History Holystal out in the free, empty space beyond the influence of Jaxx's sun ... a holystal so vast that it took our ships days to circle around it. Every facet, polished down to the finest detail, chronicled the events in the history of our planet, Jaxx's wars and triumphs, peoples, leaders, arts. ..."

Click sighed, and Rader could almost feel the icy pain in his voice. "Then I was dispatched to the Fixion Belt, assigned to construct and interpret the System Holystal here. Now I shall never see my great project finished, or even look at it again...."

Rader thought of his own brief military career, the capture of the alien supply ship, the assault on the nesting asteroid, and the Jaxxans he had killed, all leading up to a brief encore as a Deathguard. Since being turned loose in the no-man's land, he had spent much of his solitary time considering the paths that had led him here. He relived all the living he had done.

Now that he objectively reflected on his past, Rader realized he hadn't accomplished much in his years. His friendships were what he cherished most, how he and Cody wanted to do everything together, and then the close bond he had formed with his squadmates. But Cody, and his squadmates, were all dead now.

"At least you built something," Rader said. The only things his parents had received were a letter of condolence, a posthumous medal of honor, and a pension.

He realized he was consoling the alien, and the thought appalled him. He had enlisted in the League to kill roaches, Cody had died in the service, every one of his squadmates had given his life to wipe out the enemy. Rader had already killed ten Jaxxans today.

But not this one, who had used a human soldier's own med kit to try to save his soul, even though the recon scout would surely have killed Click, given the chance....

The alien was staring at him with unreadable eyes, agitated to feel the waves of emotion emanating from the

Deathguard. Rader tried to calm himself, fighting the tension so that it wouldn't activate the Werewolf Trigger. In frustration, he picked up a handful of dead soil and flung it at the rocks around them.

With a scrabbling of pebbles above, a human soldier came over the lip of the gully, sighted on the enemy, and fired without hesitation. The holystal shattered, dissolving into fragments and then nothing.

Click let out a high-pitched chittering sound as he scrambled for cover. The laser rifle followed him, and the rock wall next to his head ran molten.

The Werewolf Trigger yammered to life in Rader's head and he sprang into action before he could think, driven by the pounding command KILL, KILL! Unseen in his camouflaged Deathguard armor, he burned a neat hole through the human soldier's chest.

Click wheezed a terrified gasp and pulled himself to his feet. "Thank you."

Shock like cold water doused Rader's berserker rage, and the Werewolf Trigger fell silent inside his head.

Another soldier, the third member of the recon scout team, appeared at the top of the gully, saw his companion drop to the ground, noticed the Deathguard's laser rifle—and the huddled Jaxxan. "What the hell?"

Rader whirled, raised his laser rifle, but the scout dashed back to the safety of the rocks before the Deathguard could fire. In control now, Rader amplified his voice through the helmet, "Halt!"

He climbed up out of the loose gravel in the gulley, worked his way to higher ground in pursuit of the third soldier. But in the broken terrain with craters and a labyrinth of Jaxxan trenches, the seasoned scout had infinite places to hide. Rader looked half-heartedly, knowing the scout would head back to Base with his shocking report.

Rader returned to where Click waited, looking up at him, and the Deathguard stared at the human soldier he had just killed.

"Oh, damn! What have I done now?"

7

Tapping his fingers on the desktop (pressed fiberboard, of course—not real wood, not out here in this godforsaken asteroid belt), Commissioner Sobel pondered the news.

Very serious. An embarrassment. Incomprehensible.

One of his Deathguard had turned sour, abandoning his duty, killing two recon scouts—in the presence of an alien. Had the Deathguard been brainwashed somehow? The Jaxxans did have strange mental powers.

Or had the Deathguard suffered some kind of psychological breakdown? Sometimes, the cyborgs were so damaged mentally and physically that they were unstable, hence the impetus for turning them loose on the battlefield. Over the course of the war, four other Deathguards had failed spectacularly, and three had gone catatonic out on the front lines, where they were quickly killed.

But not a single one had ever cooperated with the enemy

before! Sobel was infuriated. They had saved the life of this—he shuffled his papers, searching for a name—this Robert Rader. Earth League cyborg engineers had taken the burned, blasted remnants of a man, patched him up enough to keep going for a final stint on the battlefield. Wasn't that what soldiers wanted?

He reviewed the records. Rader had suffered extensive damage, but he had agreed to the cyborg conversion; nothing exceptional had showed up on his psychological tests. Given a Deathguard's typically short service life, it wasn't cost-effective to waste months on extensive evaluations. The Deathguards were activated, pointed in the right direction, and turned loose on the battlefield.

As soon as the high command learned about a traitor among the lone-wolf cyborgs, however, they would crucify Sobel. The Commissioner didn't understand it. What would make the man turn against his own kind and consort with the enemy?

Sobel punched a rarely used sequence on his communications console. The viewscreen shimmered before him, as if reluctant to reveal the image of his Jaxxan counterpart.

The desiccated-looking alien's black eyes stared impatiently at him, trying to fathom the human's expression. All the roaches looked the same to Sobel but, judging by the ornamentation on the rigid hide, he ventured a guess. "Warlord Kiltik?"

When the alien tried to answer, he broke into a coughing fit before he could speak. "Commissioner Sobel? Yes, it is you."

At least the alien recognized him. "Warlord, you know I wouldn't call you if the matter wasn't urgent."

Sobel looked past the alien, gleaning details from the background of the enemy headquarters. The walls were odd planes, tilted at random in the spirit of insane Jaxxan architecture, but his eyes were drawn to a spiny mass of crystals that hung in the air behind the warlord, like a thousand fragments of glass bound up with threads of light. Some kind of three-dimensional military diagram?

He cleared his throat. "Yesterday I received some very grave news: one of my Deathguards has apparently joined with one of your soldiers. If you have subverted him somehow, hijacked his programming, the Earth League will protest strenuously. Such mental attacks are specifically prohibited in the terms of our interim treaty."

Kiltik stiffened, though Sobel couldn't read any subtle change of expression on the alien face. "We have not broken the treaty terms. I myself received reports that one of our soldiers has deserted, possibly kidnapped by a Deathguard in clear violation of our no-prisoners protocol. Summon your cyborg back to base and release our captive soldier to us so that we can address the charges of desertion."

"I can't control or recall the Deathguard, Warlord." Could it be that this wasn't a Jaxxan plan? "It seems we both have a potentially embarrassing problem. For the past few months, my record here has been impeccable, thanks in large part to the Deathguard program. I can't have one of them shooting his own comrades and fraternizing with the enemy."

Kiltik's staccato coughs interrupted his train of thought. The Warlord composed himself with an effort, then added, "Jaxxans do not break ranks. Jaxxan soldiers are tightly trained. But this deserter was not a member of the soldier caste. He was a holystal imaginer who was improperly reassigned."

Sobel didn't understand half of what the Warlord had just said, but he seized on one detail. "So, you're saying you could be in trouble for this, too."

"I have been assigned to the Fixion Belt since the beginning of the war. Although I will not lose my position here, I would prefer to avoid an 'embarrassing problem,' as you so delicately put it. My superiors will never send me back to Jaxx." He broke off for a quick burst of coughing. "However, this war was getting tedious. What do you propose we do?"

The Commissioner hid his sigh of relief. "When I received the report, I immediately sent five special commandos to terminate the defective Deathguard. I assumed your deserter would be collateral damage."

Kiltik did not sound unhappy. "Then the problem is taken care of."

"Unfortunately, the Deathguard killed the entire team, with possible assistance from his Jaxxan ally. This morning I dispatched another seven on the same mission, but they are going to have a tough time behind your lines. If you send your own hunters, one of the groups should succeed.

The Warlord stiffened. "That is nonsense, Commissioner. A ruse on your part."

Sobel hurriedly continued, "This matter concerns both of us, Warlord, and it may require all our resources to put an end to it."

The Warlord coughed once before he spoke again. "The morale of our soldier caste will suffer when they learn of this, and henceforth they will doubt the veracity of our holystal projections that guide this war. I must ponder this further and consult my holystal, Commissioner. I will contact you shortly. Your line will be open?"

"Of course." Sobel used his sweetest-sounding voice, but as soon as Kiltik's image faded, he slammed his fist on the desktop.

8

They had been on the run for days.

Before he and Click set off again, Rader had insisted on burying the other scout he had instinctively killed. He remained tense, all of his sensors alert, knowing that the third recon scout would report to Base.

With the two soldiers buried, showing a last glimmer of responsibility, Rader had activated his helmet communicator and transmitted the location of the two graves. He added a brief message to let Commissioner Sobel know he was going offline and not to expect any further reports from the field, then he tore out the locator, disengaged the built-in comm, and told Click they had to move.

The Earth League would want to deactivate and analyze Rader. It was absurd to believe he could surrender, explain what he had done, and apologize to his superiors for his mistake. That wouldn't bring the dead soldiers back to life. Now that he had proved to be dangerously unreliable as a

Deathguard, he would be "retired," and the Commissioner would quietly remove his name from the books.

And the Earth League would kill Click.

Addressing his own situation, Click was certain he would be decapitated in a public ceremony if he ever turned himself over to the Jaxxan military. They could not surrender to either side. Rader didn't know how much time he had left, but he refused to waste it. They were on their own.

On the day after Rader met Click, five Earth League trackers had found them, set up an ambush, and attacked. Click, the first to spot the trackers, set up a clumsy energy-web that knocked out one of the fighters. When the other four turned their weapons on the Jaxxan deserter, Rader let his Werewolf Trigger take over, and he eliminated them with professional efficiency.

More blood on his hands.

During Rader's training, the counselors had insisted that Deathguards had no conscience. Although he didn't think that was true, Rader did not let the guilt paralyze him. While he would not have chosen to kill other Earth League soldiers, they had given him no choice. The best solution to protect himself, and Click, and other soldiers would be to avoid any further encounters.

9

Commissioner Sobel's shuttle touched down on the Détente Asteroid's shared landing field, as had been previously arranged. It felt strange to be here at the same time as his Jaxxan counterpart. Uneasy, Sobel glanced behind him at the five specially chosen soldiers who rode in the shuttle—not as an honor guard, but as candidates for the unorthodox mission Kiltik had proposed.

It had taken Sobel some time to realize that the Jaxxan Warlord was serious; the idea proved that the alien military leader was in fact *alien*. Sobel would never have suggested such an insane approach, and yet ...

A joint team composed of both human and Jaxxan soldiers to hunt down and eliminate the two deserters as swiftly as possible? If it was a trick, then Sobel would lose five good fighters ... but he had already lost almost three times that many in his solo efforts to control the situation. He decided to risk it. This mess had to be cleaned up, swept under the rug, and the fewer people outside of Fixion who knew about it, the better.

Deathguards were the best fighters in the Earth League, although not necessarily stable or controllable, as Rader had proved. His hand-picked soldiers were specialists in their own right; Kiltik had chosen similarly talented Jaxxan hunters.

His five specialists crouched on the benches, anxiously shifting their laser rifles from hand to hand. The Commissioner had given them strict instructions not to open fire on Warlord Kiltik or any other Jaxxans when they disembarked on the Détente Asteroid. That would ignite a powderkeg, and Sobel did not want to deal with the resulting paperwork.

As the door split open and the disembarkation ramp extended, the men jumped out and stood protectively beside their Commissioner. A line of warrior caste Jaxxans greeted them, and the two groups faced each other, as if daring someone to break the agreement.

Sobel said to his team with a scowl, "Enough posturing. We've got work to do."

An alien, obviously the Warlord, walked across the landing field, sliding through the line of stiff Jaxxans. Sobel actually recognized Kiltik after only two viewscreen conversations, picking out distinctive features on the alien face.

Kiltik bowed his head, bending his stalk of neck. "Commissioner Sobel?"

"Good to meet you in person, Warlord!" He reached out to shake Kiltik's brittle hand, but the Jaxxans reacted as if it were a hostile gesture. The air thrummed with building energy-webs, and the human specialists brought their laser rifles to bear.

But the Commissioner knocked the nearest soldier's rifle

aside. "That's a friendly gesture among my people, Warlord. We're not here to kill each other now."

Kiltik stood silent, as if reading Sobel's emotions. "I sense hostility in you, but it is not directed at us. For the moment."

Sobel nodded. "I'm glad your empathic ability can break the ice."

The Warlord fought back a spasm of coughing. "Please pardon my cough—it comes from breathing this thin, dry air for years."

"No problem at all." The Commissioner gestured for his five specialists to follow him toward the normally empty embassy buildings. "Is the conference room ready? We've got important things to do."

10

______

For several days, Rader and Click made their way across the landscape, remaining hidden, staying alive, but without a plan. Each still possessed high-density ration packs, but the food would run out soon enough.

Despite the Deathguard's best attempts to remain out of sight, they were repeatedly attacked by patrols—both human and Jaxxan—eluding some, killing others.

He and Click sat together at night, quietly brooding, thinking of what they could do next. Night on Fixion was oddly different from how Rader remembered nights should be. The dark sky was strewn with brilliant clumps of asteroids from the Fixion Belt, glittering almost-moons that added to the feeble starlight. He didn't think he would ever get used to the low gravity, the thin atmosphere, the wrong constellations.

He would not see the skies of Earth again, no matter what. Even if he hadn't fallen in with Click, if he'd been a good and loyal Deathguard, he would have rampaged behind enemy lines until the alien soldiers destroyed him, or until his systems shut down from cascading failures in the cyborg process. What remained of his human body—wired up and intertwined with weapons and armor—could not withstand the shock for long. Maybe biological tissue rejection would get him, or faulty mechanical and electronic integration.

The Werewolf Trigger was oddly quiet inside his head, and he felt no compulsion to rampage among Jaxxans and slaughter them. Maybe that compass of violence had also gotten skewed, the neural hookups damaged somehow by his second thoughts. But no, it was more than that.

Each day, Click focused his thoughts and manifested the shimmering holystal. After watching his comrade's meditation, Rader had begun emulating the process as best he could. The Werewolf Trigger could send him into a murderous frenzy at any time, but he was learning to quell the urges. He hadn't known that a Deathguard could control the trigger—no one had mentioned it in his training.

Now, Click rotated and inspected the glowing image he had manifested, and even Rader could see the extreme changes in the crystal pattern. As his mistakes piled up and his options became more limited, the three-dimensional map of Click's life became more jumbled. The holystal was a sorry mess, a lump with no discernible paths leading into the future.

"We can't just stay here and hope no one finds us," Rader said. "We've got to get off of this asteroid."

During basic training with his squadmates, Rader had studied the layout of the Fixion Belt. He knew the handful of human outposts and remembered one of the first facilities the League had built here: an automated observatory on a small outlying asteroid, established before the initial encounter with Jaxxans. Observation dishes mapped the deep cosmos and monitored the Belt's other asteroids. Years ago, those telescopes had been the first to spot Jaxxan incursions into the asteroid belt, watching the aliens build their own bases on the handful of habitable rocks.

The observatory was out of the way and uninhabited, but with functional life support installed and left behind by the original construction crew.

"I know someplace safe. We'll have time and breathing space—if we can get there."

After Rader described the observatory, Click said, "But we cannot live there for long. It can only be a temporary measure."

Rader's voice was bleak. "My life is just a temporary measure. If we reach the observatory, maybe I'll stick around long enough to help you find a safer place. One step at a time. First, we've got to get from here to that little asteroid."

Click pondered for a moment. "If we need nothing more than an in-system ship to take us through the asteroids to the observatory, the Jaxxan base's landing field has many capable vessels. We could take one."

"I couldn't fly it," Rader said. "How about you?"

"That depends on the specific type of vessel. I flew several of those craft during my team's work on the System Holystal. We could try."

"We could try," Rader agreed.

Click looked across the landscape to where the distant Jaxxan base and its landing field glowed above the foreshortened horizon. Suddenly his holystal shifted, adjusted itself to the new reality—and one new bright spire emerged.

11

—————

Commissioner Sobel traveled in secret to a landing field near the main Jaxxan base, where he would meet with Warlord Kiltik. Together, they would unleash their special team behind battlefield lines to take care of the embarrassing situation before rumors could leak out.

Sobel could cover up the problem for another few days, but high command would know about it before long. He wanted to be able to announce that he'd eliminated the defective Deathguard before uncomfortable questions came down the pipeline. He didn't have much time. Although he had no understanding of Jaxxan politics or military protocol, he sensed that Kiltik felt just as much incentive and anxiety.

As he and the alien Warlord watched the ten human and Jaxxan trackers demonstrate their cooperative efforts, Kiltik startled him with an unexpected comment. "I have learned that your people call us 'cockroaches,' Commissioner."

Sobel tried to cover his embarrassment. "Roaches? Yes, I've

56

heard that. It's just an Earth insect. There are some … physical similarities."

"Not just an Earth insect, Commissioner, but one that is considered filthy, one that wallows in or feeds on garbage. In reality, the Jaxxan race is quite fastidious."

Sobel gave an unconvincing laugh. "I wouldn't worry about it. It's a common practice among grunts—er, lower level soldiers—to create derogatory names for the enemy. I'm certain your race does the same. Don't you have any insulting terms for humans?"

Warlord Kiltik twitched. "We call them *humans*. That is all the insult we need."

The ten-member hunter squad continued training. The human soldiers had already been briefed specifically on how to kill a Deathguard (details they would not reveal to their alien counterparts). The current exercises showed the team members how to effectively combine Earth League laser weaponry and Jaxxan energy-web techniques. Most impor-tantly, they got used to working with one another. That was the big barrier to break.

Kiltik said, "I find it discouraging that ten trained fighters are necessary to combat two deserters."

"No one is more annoyed than I am, but those two have already killed fourteen of my fighters and six of yours. I should be proud of our Deathguard's fighting skills, but I cannot help but wonder if your soldier somehow corrupted him."

Kiltik choked his dry, rustling cough. "Who corrupted whom? Remember, Jaxxans are empaths. How can one of us possibly remain normal when constantly bombarded with your Deathguard's alien perspectives? Our deserter was already flawed, in the wrong place after being removed from the System Holystal project. Your Deathguard has irreparably damaged him."

A Jaxxan trotted up from one of the outpost buildings and handed the Warlord a small geometric crystal. Kiltik turned the object over in his hands, feeling the facets and reading its shape. When he finished, the crystal vanished from his hands.

"I have just been informed by my reconnaissance that the two deserters were spotted in the wastelands, moving away from the front. Then they vanished again."

Sobel frowned. "If we knew where they were going, our hunter squad could intercept them."

The Commissioner remembered visiting Rader in the med-center when he was no more than a few mangled lumps of flesh wired up to life-support; he'd had high hopes for his newest Deathguard. Now, he just wanted him removed from the equation.

He and Kiltik stood together, admiring their special team.

<hr>

HIGH ABOVE THE ECLIPTIC, bright starlight reflected off of the giant planes of polished cometary ice and majestic crystal spires being assembled there by Jaxxan imaginers and psychics.

The human military did not know the location of the System Holystal construction above the asteroid belt. Even if they did stumble upon the site, they wouldn't understand it. Warlord Kiltik did not understand it himself. Holystal interpretation was not the duty of his caste, but he trusted the skills and knowledge of those who manifested such a representation. They could read the lines of fate, the fractures and angles that showed which paths Jaxxans could take into the future.

Thousands of workers operated here in space. While high-powered imaginers used their mental powers to create holographic portions of the ever-changing structure, teams of builders pushed small chunks of orbiting ice and diverted comets to deliver the materials here.

The Jaxxan race now inhabited five star systems. In each one, a revered System Holystal such as this one guided their decisions. The Jaxxan deserter who had joined forces with the human Deathguard had once been a skilled holystal imaginer who could understand subtle nuances in the cosmic constructions.

Now the Warlord flew in a small observation shuttle, piloted by his chief adviser. It was part of Kiltik's regular briefing to plan the next week's tactics, but he was losing confidence in the adviser's recommendations. Any decent interpreter should have been able to warn against the current mess. The chief adviser knew his failing and desperately wanted to return to the Warlord's good graces.

The observation shuttle approached the gigantic holystal, and Kiltik marveled at its facets, saw the distant starlight that reflected from the shining surfaces. He realized that it had been a mistake to demote the holystal engineer and turn him into a mere battlefield soldier. Observing the facets and angles, the Warlord could see how easy it would be to predict a different future from all the complexity. Even his chief adviser now suspected that some of the deserter's contradictory warnings might have had some merit.

However, the deserter's actions were indefensible: collaborating with a human—and not just any human, but a Deathguard who was single-handedly responsible for the murder of dozens if not hundreds of Jaxxan soldiers! It was shameful, an embarrassment, and Warlord Kiltik needed the situation resolved. In that, he was completely aligned with his human counterpart.

Reticent and chastised, the chief adviser flew the survey shuttle in a tight orbit over the giant holystal. Kiltik remained silent, his disapproval hanging in the enclosed cockpit. The adviser devoted his attention to the kaleidoscopic facets, the ever-changing fissures, crystalline angles, cracks and impurities, each of which indicated a different future, a path of fate that must be heeded.

Finally, the Warlord expressed his impatience. "I am not sightseeing. I am here to ferret out information. You are my interpreter. If you wish to regain my respect, then find answers." He turned his polished eyes to the nervous chief adviser. "Look at the holystal, find the portions that are relevant to these deserters. I need to know what their plans are. Our hunter squad must know where they intend to go."

The adviser's voice was thin and warbling. "The holystal is still under construction, Warlord. Even if we find the proper facets, any answers are merely within a locus of possibilities."

"Then I need those possibilities. Narrow them down so I can make my decisions."

The chief adviser guided the survey shuttle over an expanse of stalagmite-covered ice and broken shards, a jumble that meant something to a Jaxxan properly versed in interpretation. "There, Warlord!" The adviser pointed to a flurry of cracks and warped transparency in the polished ice. "That appeared since my last visit here."

"What changed?"

"The deserters have made a concrete plan, which is reflected here. This allows us to draw conclusions."

Kiltik was careful not to praise the man too much. "How accurate can you be?"

"I have a ... reasonable certainty." He was cautious, not wanting to commit to what might be another error. The chief adviser stared through the windowport, assessing the ripples and distortion in the crystalline structure. "We cannot extrapolate far into the future, but I can project where they intend to go next."

Kiltik felt pleased. "If that information is accurate enough for our hunter squad to intercept them, then we won't need any further projections."

12

———

With Click leading the way, they entered the hulking lump of buildings that was the Jaxxan military base—neatly organized but crowded structures, large and small, with flat walls slanted at hard-to-interpret angles. The buildings were dark, the passages between them narrow, the architecture strange and disorienting to Rader—everything based on oblique angles rather than perpendicular walls.

The Jaxxan military base, as with the human outpost on the other side of Fixion, had started out as a basic forward station, a testing ground for a possible colony, before the war broke out. But no hopeful colonists had ever arrived, and now the temporary city was a bizarre collage of trading posts, refectories, warehouses, arsenals, administrative hives, and command posts.

He and Click had to make their way through the middle of it at night, skirt any populated sections, and reach the landing field, where they hoped to steal a small in-system craft.

Rader used his suit sensors to scan for danger, while coaching Click in how to keep himself from being seen. Somehow, the alien couldn't grasp the technique of searching for cover. However, after countless switchbacks and false starts, Click had become lost in the tangled streets. He sounded dismayed. "I was assigned to the System Holystal project out in space. I spent very little time in this settlement."

Rader scanned ahead. "We'll figure out a viable route to the landing field." He and his companion moved from alley to alley until they had lost all sense of direction.

Disoriented and impatient, Click stepped into a wide intersection to get his bearings while Rader took a reading to determine how far they were from the ships. The Deathguard's sensors detected movement in the shadows, forms converging on them with high-sensitivity detectors of their own. He knew this wasn't right.

He heard a voice hiss, a *human* voice, here in the middle of the Jaxxan base. "That's him! The Deathguard—and the deserter!"

A laser rifle etched a molten line across the flat tan wall of a nearby building. Rader jerked Click back into the dark alley as a freshly formed green energy-web hurtled toward them. The shimmering threads sliced off the corner of a structure.

The hunters surged out of their cover, humans *and Jaxxans* tracking them together. Before Rader could grasp the implications, he used his laser rifle to kill one—a Jaxxan, he thought—and scatter the others. *One down.* Synthetic adrenaline juiced him, and he fell into full defensive mode. He dragged Click with him down to the end of the alley and blasted a hole through the thin wall so they could push their way into a side street.

They dashed through the maze of passageways, glad for the darkness. Deathguard reflexes kicked in, filling him with a sense of heightened danger. Without saying a word, Click ran along beside him, in shock. From behind, they could hear shouts and noises as the hunter squad continued their pursuit.

Rader was amazed to realize that the Earth League and the Jaxxan military had cooperated to hunt them down. It would take all his skills and energy to avoid capture and keep Click alive. He focused entirely on their escape.

Suddenly his insides jerked, and he felt pressure building up in his brain as the Werewolf Trigger activated: KILL. KILL.

"Click, get out of here!"

The Jaxxan stumbled next to him. "But where should I go?"

"I'm dangerous! Get away from *me!*" Rader shoved him off to one side, hunching over in his futile attempts to control himself. "Quick, dammit!" Click stumbled off, running but woefully clumsy.

The Deathguard's implanted weapons systems activated, his laser rifle became part of him, and his head exploded with red noise, the alarm voice pounding against pressure points in his brain.

The whole world around him became a target, and the enemy lost its distinct form. He didn't know for sure what it was he must KILL, but he had to KILL it anyway. The berserker alarm told him to.

Gripping his laser rifle with reinforced gloves, he leaped out into the street, taking pot-shots at buildings, shooting at shadows in windows. Rader's shout was amplified by his helmet speakers—and from his scream, the hunter squad pinpointed his location.

He looked ahead down an alley, studying details through light-amplification sensors. A vague memory jumped into his mind. Someone had gone that way, indistinct—the enemy? He bounded between the angled buildings, paying no heed to the movement behind him.

Rader breathed with mechanical rhythm, peering into the shadows with heightened senses. His cyborg systems increased his metabolism, supercharged what remained of his biological tissue.

A brilliant shooting star, gift from the Fixion Belt, whistled over his head in a final flash of glory.

Rader leaped forward, unable to control his actions. He saw a Jaxxan ahead of him, running, stumbling along. A vague, distant voice tugged at the back of his mind, telling him that this wasn't the real enemy ... but the Werewolf Trigger drowned the rational voice.

Click.

The lone Jaxxan let out a chitter of fear and ran along a perpendicular alley, straight toward the landing field, still trying to reach the ship they needed. He reached an open construction area where skeletons of oddly angled buildings stood among piles of naked plastic-alloy girders.

Rader launched himself into the construction area like a jungle fighter. Shadows surrounded him, but he paid them no heed. Ahead, he saw the alien, the enemy. Recognition flickered in his mind for a moment—but the clamor forced it away.

KILL

No!

Click stumbled among tangled wires and slabs of polymer concrete in piles for assembly crews. He stopped short against a half-constructed wall, wheezing in the thin air.

Rader stepped victoriously over a girder, then leaped down in front of the cornered target. He pushed the laser rifle close to the Jaxxan's large black eyes.

But the alien refused to use his energy-web. Click merely regarded the weapon's blunt barrel.

KILL KILL, the voice of the Werewolf Trigger insisted.

No! *No!*

Rader's will struggled against a fortune of scientific conditioning. He had to fire, had to destroy. The command pulled harder at his mind, building in intensity, tearing him apart.

KILL KILL

No!

The Deathguard swung his weapon up and went wild, blasting buildings, slicing through support struts, destroying anything but Click.

Jumping away, he charged back in the direction he had come—and ran abruptly into the hunter squad. They reacted, but the Deathguard was too fast. The Werewolf Trigger ordered him to KILL—and this time he didn't resist. He left two dead human soldiers and one Jaxxan in the wake of his fury, then dove into cover, racing through the construction site. *Four down.*

The six remaining members of the hunter squad took only a second to regroup. Leaving the three bodies where they had fallen, one of the Jaxxans motioned to the others, and they stalked after the Deathguard.

As soon as he escaped the scattered hunters, the Werewolf Trigger lapsed into quiescence, and Rader's thoughts, intelligence, self-control flooded back into his mind.

He heard shouts from behind as the hunters called to one

another. They were still out of sight, but with his amplified senses, he could hear them split up to approach him from different directions. However, Rader had an advantage now as calm calculation returned to him. The others expected him to act like a rampaging berserker.

He had to damp his emotions, draw them back into himself so that his turmoil wouldn't become a beacon that declared his hidden presence to the empathic Jaxxans. Rader sought refuge in the darkness beneath an outside stairway, and his non-reflective, camouflage armor helped him melt into the shadows, turning him into a shadow himself.

He breathed methodically, forcing rigid control back into his body, imitating Click's holystal meditation. Click! He didn't *think* he had killed his comrade. Rader closed his eyes, ignoring the marching feet and hushed voices that hurried closer, then moved past him.

When the team had passed, he emerged from his sanctuary. Instead of pursuing the hunters, he crept toward the landing field and their way off Fixion. Click would have gone to the ships—he hoped.

Across twenty meters of open concrete, a small short-range cargo vessel rested, as well as six larger personnel transports and a bulbous fuel tanker. One lonely Jaxxan guard stood at the open door of the small cargo ship.

On the perimeter of the landing field, Rader spotted Click's ill-concealed form in the shadow of a building. At least the alien was trying. The Deathguard silently made his way over to his friend, keeping so well concealed that even Click didn't know he was there until the last moment.

The Jaxxan froze, then realized that he no longer sensed

the raging, killing beast inside the Deathguard. Rader spoke in a whisper. "I'm in control now, but the rest of that squad is still after us. It won't be long before they realize I've doubled back. Let's get that ship!"

He knew that if they could get off of Fixion, they could lose themselves in the debris of the asteroid belt, travel slowly, hopscotch from rock to rock, and reach the observatory asteroid. Beyond that, Rader didn't care.

He brought his laser rifle up, aimed. "I'll get rid of the sentry."

But Click's bony arm stopped him. "Wait, there is a better way." He hunkered down and concentrated on the sentry. Even through his armor, Rader felt a tingle in the air; his sensors registered an energy buildup. A galaxy of lights flickered in the deep universe of Click's black eyes.

The sentry flailed his angular arms as a half-formed energy-web folded over him. The sentry clawed at the dimly sparkling strands, searching for his unseen attacker—a Jaxxan attacker.

Leaving their hiding place, Rader and Click rushed across the landing field toward the Jaxxan cargo ship. When Click spoke to the sentry, Rader was surprised to hear the menace in his comrade's usually timid voice. "Do nothing unwise, or I shall be forced to complete my web."

The Jaxxan guard did nothing unwise.

While Rader kept his laser rifle pointed at the sentry, Click scuttled forward and activated the hatch. "Can you fly this ship?"

The insectoid head bobbed up and down on its stalk of a neck.

"A hostage and a pilot," Rader said. "Good enough." He did

not know what they would do with the sentry once they reached their destination.

Click chittered his instructions to the sentry. "You will fly on a random, evasive course. The humans have an observatory asteroid located on the far edge of the Belt. It must be in the database."

Rader detected movement in the construction area, the hunter squad picking up on them again. "They're coming. Get inside the ship—now!"

With a victorious outcry, the hunters charged across the landing field. Rader shoved Click through the cargo ship's open hatch as one of the human soldiers braced for a careful shot, but chose the wrong Jaxxan. He burned a large hole in the alien sentry's back.

As he tried to escape, Rader's left leg suddenly collapsed, and he sprawled on the ramp. The attackers raced toward them, shouting, and he rolled, trying to assess the damage, sure that a laser blast had cut through the armor, ruined his cyborg leg systems. Using his good leg, his elbows, and his gloves, he hauled himself to the hatch.

Click had turned back to help him, and an energy-web glittered against the hull, smoking and sparking. Rader yelled, "Leave me—get to the control room!"

Instead, the Jaxxan grabbed his arms, dragged him the rest of the way into the ship. As soon as he was clear, Click sealed the hatch.

Rader looked down to see how much damage the shot had done to his leg, but he saw no burned hole, no melted slag of armor or shorted-out cyborg parts. The leg had simply failed.

Click dashed away from the hatch and scrambled up a

thin-runged ladder to the control deck. Rader called after him, "You *can* fly this type of ship, can't you?"

Click pointedly did not answer, and Rader stifled a groan.

THE CARGO SHIP ROSE JERKILY, leaving behind a whirlpool of displaced air. The hunter squad watched in anger and defeat. After the vessel zigzagged in a drunkard's flight from the landing field, the soldiers watched the flares of its engines dwindle into Fixion's thin atmosphere.

The human captain stared at the sentry who lay sprawled on the still-warm pavement. "He's dead. We can't interrogate him for any intel the two deserters might have revealed."

The Jaxxan leader shook his head. "Not too late. We will implement a post-mortem interrogation."

He removed equipment from his belt pack—a probe, a diagnostic reader, two long wires, and a skull splitter. Jamming down hard, he broke the chitinous shell of the dead sentry's head, spreading the hard faceplates to expose the soft, contoured brain. "We should still be able to access the chemical memory of the last few moments he experienced."

The Jaxxan unfolded the screen, then dipped the sharp probe wires into the dead alien brain. Static washed across the screen accompanied by surreal images, colored patterns, old memories. He worked quickly before the memory-storage chemicals dissipated, the neurons deteriorated.

He touched different sections of tissue with the probe wires, moving urgently, until he found a blurred image of Deathguard Rader and his Jaxxan companion. He zeroed in, turned up the volume on the receiver, and heard their words, relived their last conversation, studied everything they had said.

The Jaxxan captain got the information he needed before the chemical traces crumbled into disjointed fragments and incomplete sentences. It was enough. He looked up at his comrades. "Now we know where they are going."

13

"They got past *all ten?*" Sobel was still rubbing sleep from his eyes in front of the image of Kiltik.

The insistent call from the viewscreen had dragged him out of bed. He hadn't expected to be disturbed, but Sobel had given the Jaxxan Warlord his direct contact code. At first, the Commissioner thought he would be happy to receive the call regardless of the hour, expecting good news—but Kiltik had not told him what he wanted to hear.

"Yes, all ten, Commissioner. The Deathguard killed four of them and escaped with the Jaxxan soldier in a stolen ship. A very reckless flight, evasive action. They vanished into the asteroid field."

"Good riddance," Sobel muttered, but knew the problem didn't end there. Even if the two were never seen again—and the cyborg systems had to start breaking down soon—Sobel's failure to resolve the situation properly would be a permanent blot on his record. He couldn't just let the Deathguard die on his own. "This is a disaster, Warlord. We'll never be able to track them—unless you can guess their destination from the patterns in that holystal thing of yours?"

The Jaxxan's face was unreadable. "We have a clearer answer than that. Your Deathguard and my deserter tried to take one of the landing-field sentries hostage, but our hunter squad shot him inadvertently—a happy accident. Fortunately, one of my soldiers set up a mind probe quickly enough. We know the location of the asteroid where the two intend to go."

"Really?" Sobel didn't quite allow himself a sigh of relief. "Well, that's better than a complete debacle, but we have to act without delay. Let me send you two of my best fighterships— ours are faster than yours."

"Accepted." An expression of what might have been humor crossed Kiltik's face, but then the alien broke into a spasm of dry coughing.

Sobel rolled his tongue around in his dry mouth. He had been asleep for only a few hours, and already his mouth tasted foul. "I'll get those fighterships sent over right away—and please don't shoot at them! Then I'm going back to bed." He yawned, but felt no better for it. "Don't you ever sleep?"

"No."

"Oh ... Well, I'll speak to you when I have something to report, Warlord."

"Call me Kiltik." The Warlord touched the screen, and the images of his fingertips were blurred. "Now that I have met you in person, I find this communication very unsatisfactory. I feel no emotions, which makes understanding more difficult. From now on, I would rather dispense with this apparatus and meet you face-to-face."

"That can be arranged—but let's hope we can wrap up this problem quickly." He blanked the screen, then established another connection. He spoke to a corporal in the fightership hangars, repeated his baffling instructions several times, then worked his way up the chain of command.

Sobel knew his bed would be very cold by the time he finally climbed back into it.

14

They flew away from Fixion, diving at breakneck speed and without a course into the scramble of drifting asteroids. Click quickly became adept at maneuvering the cargo shuttle.

"The military will be tracking us. We have to get far enough away," he announced over the intercom.

Rader still lay on the lower deck, trying to get his uncooperative leg to function. He was sure the survivors of the hunter squad would be commandeering their own pursuit ships. Click accelerated as much as he could tolerate, and his tough alien body could withstand severe gravitational stresses. Rader's Deathguard armor protected him.

"Once we are in the densest portion of the Belt, I will cut the engines," Click continued. "Then our signature becomes identical to that of the other small asteroids."

Taking a moment to assess his own malfunctions, Rader propped himself against a bulkhead. The cyborg leg had suffered no obvious damage, but the neural pulses from his brain no longer made it move as he intended. Unavoidable glitches, the start of what would be a cascade of breakdowns, and he knew how to do only the most basic repairs. He breathed silent thanks that his systems had functioned long enough and well enough to get him and Click off of Fixion. Now, if he could only find a plan that would get his Jaxxan comrade to safety.

One problem at a time.

Working with enforced patience, still feeling the afterwash of the synthetic adrenaline that had poured through his systems, Rader removed emergency tools, cracked open the primary circuits, and performed a standard reset procedure twice before his armored leg would twitch again. He swung himself back to his feet and tried to walk. He took painstaking steps at first, then limped forward. The metal ladder to the upper deck proved quite a challenge, but he eventually made his way into the control chamber.

Click flew the ship among a cluster of high-albedo icy asteroids. To confuse any systems tracking them, he matched the orbits of random stony asteroids of approximately the same size as the cargo ship, and the glaring sunlight masked their thermal signature after Click shut down the engines.

"We wait half a day," the Jaxxan said, "then alter course slightly to take us closer to the observatory asteroid. We are patient."

"Yes, patient." Rader silently ran thorough diagnostic checks of his systems, his power sources, the alignment of neural conduits, and found many domino-effect malfunctions; his last battle and escape in the Jaxxan base had strained his components, running out the service life. "Take as much time as you need."

One way or another, he doubted he had more than a week. Click didn't need to know that, but his empathic senses would probably tell him anyway.

"With the ship's life-support levels, we can survive for three days. Breathe as little as possible."

Rader realized it was a joke. "Nobody's been to the observatory asteroid in ages. Better hope their systems are functional. We won't make it to anywhere else."

Click said, "We have nowhere else to go."

"That's the next thing I have to figure out."

While they drifted, Rader tried to implement repairs to his cyborg systems in order to buy a little extra time, but most of the systems were beyond him. And the failings were in his mental interface, not in the large-scale mechanics. He experienced a persistent headache that seemed to be growing worse. His eyesight suffered from double vision, as if the images from his real eye and artificial eye did not align properly.

For two days, they made their cautious, tedious journey across a stepping-stone course. Click monitored the cargo ship's passive sensors. They were surrounded by far too many datapoints, which was good—a swarm like identical needles in a very large haystack. "I see no indication that pursuers have followed us through the numerous blips."

Rader's hope grew as the image of the observatory asteroid grew on the viewscreen before him. It was a domed rock less than two kilometers wide, moving among the rubble in the Fixion Belt. In less than an hour, if Click kept up his improved navigational abilities, they would arrive.

Rader almost smiled for the first time since ... since that final day with his squadmates. He should have died then, and *that* day could have served as his final flash of glory, not this awkward encore. With so much time to think aboard their ship, he could not escape the conclusion. Even after they reached the observatory, Click had little chance of going much farther. He had not managed to come up with a viable plan.

He felt dismayed that this abortive "second chance" as a Deathguard had accomplished nothing—not for himself, not for his people, not for Click either. It was just a delay. And when Rader's cyborg systems finally broke down, Click was not likely to last long alone on the observatory asteroid. He'd wait there until food supplies and life support ran out, like a man stranded on a desert island.

Short-term thinking. But it was better than *shorter*-term thinking. They were still alive. Rader had to hope they would find some other ship, or supplies ... or a miracle once they got to the asteroid.

In the pilot seat, Click seemed satisfied. If he detected Rader's troubled thoughts, he did not show it.

As they made their final approach, Rader studied the enhanced images, saw the framework of bowl-shaped radio telescopes reflecting starlight, the automated tracking mirrors of optical telescopes gazing out into the universe to gather astronomical data.

And he saw the recently installed military fuel depot, large tanks of spacecraft fuel, as well as Earth League stockpiled missiles, a forest of javelin-shaped warheads ready to be launched. He stared, realizing that this asteroid was not as forgotten and abandoned as he had hoped.

When Click scanned the rear navigational sensors, his glassy black eyes clouded over. "Rader ..."

Two pursuit fighterships swept up behind them like

cruising sharks. They came straight toward the sluggish Jaxxan cargo ship.

"I cannot accelerate enough to outrun them," Click said. "And we have very little fuel remaining."

Rader glanced at the type of ship, knew their capabilities. "Those are the League's fastest fighterships. We don't have any chance of outrunning them."

When the pair of pursuers circled the cargo ship, Rader saw the Earth League insignia, but the image blurred and shimmered in his unfocused vision. The face that appeared on the comm screen, though, was a Jaxxan, demanding their surrender.

"Why don't they just destroy us from a distance?" Click said.

"They will want proof—or trophies."

The squad of hunters was composed of humans and Jaxxans working together; Rader wondered if the Earth League soldiers had orders to kill their alien comrades after a successful mission—especially now that they had seen the unexpected missile stockpile hidden on the observatory asteroid. Commissioner Sobel could not possibly want the Jaxxan high command to know about the depot.

"We cannot defend ourselves," Click said. "This cargo shuttle has no weapons."

Rader held his laser rifle. "We can defend ourselves."

A clang of metal thrummed through the hull as the two fighterships attached to the Jaxxan airlocks. "I have sealed the airlocks and denied them access," Click said.

"They'll burn their way through." On the visual monitors he discerned a glow on the inner hull: one airlock being cut away by a powerful laser rifle, and the opposite lock rippling from a continuously applied energy-web. Even a Deathguard couldn't defend both hatches at the same time.

Limping on his faulty leg, aligning his weapons systems with the vision from only his artificial eye to minimize errors, Rader picked a defensible position at the entrance to the cargo ship's cockpit. He braced himself there, holding his laser rifle ready, his targeting sensors attuned. His artificial heart pumped nutrients through his cyborg and biological components, but the Werewolf Trigger remained silent. He didn't need it. Or maybe that, too, had malfunctioned.

Both hatches surrendered at the same time, and on the visual monitors he watched the remaining members of the hunter squad move with brisk efficiency through the corridors up to the cockpit. The humans were wearing mirrored armor, which would reflect the beam of his laser rifle.

"I'll take out as many as I can, but I doubt I'll get them all," he said. "Sorry we didn't make it all the way."

"We made it this far, Rader, and now we are dead." Click's voice was strangely emotionless. "But so are they."

Rader identified an expression on the alien face that no other human would have seen. Click punched a sequence into the navigational computer, and the observatory asteroid shifted its position in front of them. "Our engines cannot outrun the fighterships, but we have enough power to drag them along."

Rader nodded approval. "A Deathguard's mission is to cause mayhem."

"Yes, I believe we have caused a fair amount of mayhem," Click said.

"I just wish we had accomplished something more than that." He wondered if the Commissioner would take the medal of honor away from his family ... but that would be admitting something had gone wrong.

The six members of the hunter squad advanced up to the control deck.

Rader darted a farewell glance at his comrade. After setting their collision course, Click crouched in motionless silence, not even trying to fight. Instead, he hunched over a shining image, studying his last holystal. The glowing shape was a dazzling, perfect sphere.

Rader took a quick breath. "What does that mean?"

"It means that we have run out of alternatives."

The hunter squad let out a chorus of shouts as they stormed the final corridor. Rader opened fire, placing a neat, centimeter-wide hole through the head of one Jaxxan.

Now the Werewolf Trigger clamored in his mind, but as he fired on the advancing squad members, his arm jerked and spasmed, spoiling his aim. The Jaxxans took shelter against door wells in the corridor, and Rader's energy blasts reflected off the mirrored armor, ricocheting down the hall. The fractured beams dissipated, but he kept firing.

Rader's leg gave out beneath him, and he tumbled over like a mannequin. He tried to aim his laser rifle as momentum carried his body in a clumsy roll, and he lay face up on the deck.

An energy-web hurled by the two remaining Jaxxans engulfed Click in luminous tangles. Click cried out as the web completed itself, but his words turned to scintillating shards of sound. His holystal dwindled to a last spark of light until that, too, vanished.

The human fighters targeted the Deathguard and rushed forward, while the Jaxxans ran past him, urgently trying to reach the shuttle controls in time. Rader stared at them through his visor: A band of humans and aliens working together, to destroy a human and alien who had dared to work together. He wondered if they understood the irony.

He looked past them to the cockpit to see the observatory asteroid rushing toward them. The cargo shuttle was going to crash into the spiny missile batteries instead of the tele-scopes ... not that it made any difference.

A short time was better than no time—and he had spent it with a friend rather than alone.

15

S obel grinned, ready to celebrate the news. "Well, Kiltik
—we did it!"

"Yes, not even one of your Deathguards could
resist the two of us." The Warlord sat across from him in the
conference room on the Détente Asteroid. Kiltik had shuttled
over to the Earth League embassy at Sobel's invitation, so they
could await the final report.

The Warlord seemed troubled, however. The Commissioner would never have noticed it before, but now he could
detect subtle differences in the alien's moods. "You don't seem
as overjoyed as I expected."

"Perhaps I grieve for the loss of your ... astronomical
facility."

"Oh, that!" Sobel brushed the matter aside. "It was obso-
lete. We can always build another one—astronomy is low on
our priorities."

"But it did provide a good hiding place for your weapons

stockpile. Either astronomy is quite a volatile science, or your supposed observatory was merely a camouflage."

Sobel felt flustered and embarrassed, especially in his moment of great victory. "I could lie about that, but you'd be able to detect the truth, wouldn't you?"

"Yes." For his own part, unfortunately, Sobel couldn't tell whether the Jaxxan was lying. The Warlord said, "We will need to discuss this further—at the appropriate time."

"I'd be happy to talk about it with you, but right now, this calls for a drink! Would you care for some refreshment?"

The Jaxxan rattled his dry cough. "Water would be nice."

"Nothing more festive?" Sobel frowned. "As you wish, Warlord." He placed ice cubes in a glass and filled it from a pitcher.

Kiltik broke out in a spasm of raspy coughing. Sobel ran to help him. "You really should have that cough taken care of. Would you like one of my medics to check you out?"

The Jaxxan breathed deeply, expressing his thanks. "No, it would do no good. The dry air of Fixion has ruined my health. I have spent years in this climate—it is a wonder I'm still alive, so far from home." In a distant, dreamy voice, Kiltik described his warm humid planet with steaming jungles and crystal cities, where rain fell in syrupy drops and sluggish rivers were choked with sweet algae.

Sobel tried to picture it. "After our great victory over the two deserters, can't you use the political mileage to request a transfer back to Jaxx? For a short while at least?"

"I do not plan to report this matter to my superiors at all. I will be here for the duration of the war." He looked up. "How long are you to be stationed here?"

"I have a year and a half left of my three years."

"A year and a half." Kiltik sipped his cold water. "These facilities on the Détente Asteroid are used ineffectively." He paused for a long moment. "Would it be possible for me to visit you from time to time, friend Sobel?"

Still deciding what his celebratory drink would be, the Commissioner finally sat down with his own glass of ice water. "That could be arranged." He chuckled. "Friend Kiltik."

ESCAPE HATCH

1

The mass of alien tentacles writhed over the side of the Earth Planetary Navy destroyer. When the *Far Horizon*'s Admiral Bruce Haldane saw the vicious things crash onto the deck and scatter in all directions, he knew the battle was lost. There was no stopping the swarm of Sluggos.

Rough seas rocked the destroyer, but the grim crew who manned the guns against the worm things were not worried about getting seasick.

The enormous cluster of alien creatures also attacked from beneath the surface, hammering the *Far Horizon*'s armored hull. The thunderous clang was even louder than the explosive artillery. *How could something so soft and squishy sound so loud?* he wondered, then stalked along the deck, a weapon in each hand as he shot the swarming slugs. Each creature exploded with a disgusting splat of oozing protoplasm. The ship's crew were running up and down the open deck, wading through smashed Sluggos, but the things kept coming from below.

Unstoppable.

Each alien was the length and thickness of Haldane's forearm, looking like a beige banana slug with teeth. The Sluggos combined and moved in concert, wrapping their wormlike bodies together to form a larger organism. Thousands of Sluggos braided into a giant tentacle that rose up from the rough seas to wrap around the destroyer, and then dissolving into countless ravenous components again. The Sluggos squirmed forward, mouths chomping. They were blind, but they were hungry, and there were so many of them that the doomed crew had no place to hide.

Admiral Haldane was grim, but he drove back his panic. As their leader, he had to focus on the fight. His crew was yelling, some clearly fearful because they had just begun to realize they were all going to die. They didn't have an escape hatch. Knowing he could give his all and still live to fight another day let Haldane concentrate on the crisis and do what was necessary, without being crippled by fear of his own mortality.

"Keep shooting! By God, there's no shortage of targets!"

The lower decks had been infested, and evacuating sailers had come out into the open. One of the nearby seamen, his dungarees splotched with yellow-green ichor and bright red blood, fired his sidearm until it was empty, then snatched another still-hot weapon from the hands of a dying seaman on the deck. The wounded seaman's abdomen had been ripped open, and his guts spilled out like another swarm of Sluggos. Without pause, the desperate seaman continued firing, each bullet exploding one—or more—of the squirming aliens.

"Aye, sir. It's not a shortage of targets we're worried about, Admiral," he shouted over his shoulder. "It's running out of ammo."

Haldane kept firing his own sidearm, not even making a dent in the invasion. He shouted back, hoping he sounded encouraging, "According to the weapons locker manifest, we should have ten thousand rounds aboard the *Far Horizon*." The number sounded impressive, objectively, but not in comparison to the million hungry Sluggos swarming over the destroyer. He had opened the armory and distributed weapons as widely and as swiftly as possible, to the Marines as well as to any other sailor with fingers and thumbs.

Everyone aboard would be alien food before long. Haldane felt sorry for them, but he'd make sure they got a nice memorial ceremony back in La Diego.

After humanity had ventured away from Earth and set up fledgling colonies on the Moon, Mars, and the asteroid belt, nobody ever guessed that an alien invasion would target Earth's oceans. The invaders had landed in the Pacific, emerged from their interstellar spaceships, and began swarming through the seas.

The slimy creatures moved like a gigantic school of fish, thousands of separate pieces that formed a sentient community organism—an incomprehensible alien creature that managed to build starships, travel across space, to plunge into Earth's oceans, where they reproduced at a furious pace— whether by fission, or breeding, or eggs, no one knew—and swiftly became a terrible hazard.

They attacked ships, sinking commercial freighters, cruise liners, fishing vessels. The Earth Planetary Navy was little more than a token force, peacekeepers and emergency responders. It had been a long time since battle fleets went on a full-scale war footing. Now, the EPN went on the hunt, combing the waters in search of the enemy.

Sonar could detect the large clusters of Sluggos, which then vanished with each pulse and then re-formed elsewhere. Admiral Haldane had already led two preliminary engagements, each one disastrous. He was about to make it three for three.

Reaching this point in the South Pacific, the suspected location of the original Sluggo starships, the *Far Horizon* had dropped dozens of depth pulsers hoping to destroy the underwater alien base. The explosions had been wonderful, creating rooster-tails of water like massive geysers. The shock waves should have ruined any Sluggo structures on the ocean floor.

The excitement was short-lived, though. The individual aliens had combined into a monstrous body, countless squirming components adding together like cells. Then the community organism rose up like the most twisted nightmare of any sailor's legend and attacked the *Far Horizon*.

The shapeless beast shifted and rearranged its bodily blueprint, first engulfing the destroyer with tentacles and then smashing onto the deck in a huge flat mass like a manta, which then dissolved into an overwhelming slimy army of individual Sluggos that could attack—and devour.

Constant gunfire continued to ring out, and even ten thousand rounds didn't last very long. When the crew ran out of ammo, they used metal pipes, tools, even small storage pods, to smash the things. Someone had rigged a flamethrower and jetted fire that fried the wormlike aliens. When their protoplasm boiled, they exploded, but the Sluggos did not feel pain or fear, and more of them came forward. One young seaman thrashed as a dozen of the worm-things chewed into the meat of his thighs and calves, then tunneled through his chest. He kept screaming until one crawled down his throat.

Other seamen had better luck with fire extinguishers, driving the Sluggos away, briefly, but there was no place to hide. Each extinguisher ran out within minutes, and the crew used the empty tanks to smash more Sluggos.

"Turn the heavy-caliber guns down," Haldane yelled. "Fire into the water!"

"But, sir, that'll do nothing!"

"It'll make some big explosions," he shouted back. That was something at least.

At central fire control, weapons officers tilted the large-bore the guns down, and the guns roared, but even the heavy shells did little more than stir up the Sluggos in the water. In response, a huge pseudopod composed of braided Sluggos lurched up, wavered in the air just long enough for Haldane to estimate the tens of thousands of hungry creatures that comprised it, then it dissociated in midair, creating a rain of hungry Sluggos that fell onto the *Far Horizon*.

Haldane had found shelter under the bridge wing, but he watched the crew get slaughtered. He had emptied both of his sidearms, and he had no other defenses but his bare hands and his boot heels. The squirming aliens came at him like an unstoppable invertebrate tide. . . .

No one in the EPN had had more direct experience with the Sluggos than Admiral Bruce Haldane. He had studied their movements firsthand in three engagements now, seen how they attacked. He made mental notes. Even though he didn't understand what he saw, his knowledge was irreplaceable. If Earth was going to win this war against the undersea invasion, *he* had to survive.

The overburdened destroyer was groaning, listing to starboard, clearly taking on water from belowdecks. The pounding Sluggos had chewed and torn through the lower hull and were even now swarming through the breach, infesting the ship even faster than seawater could fill it. Damage control crews had been devoured as they rushed to respond. The destroyer was going down.

As he backed against the bulkhead, he watched hundreds of Sluggos burst through the hatches, huge maggots writhing up the ladders and spilling onto the deck. Even with the din of gunfire, explosions, and shouts, Haldane could hear them moving around in the compartments below, feasting.

Then they came toward him.

Most of the *Far Horizon*'s crew had been slaughtered already, but Haldane stood straight and proud, facing the alien enemy. He owed it to the brave men and women who perished here: He would stay until the very last as the hordes of fleshy bodies and chewing mouths squirmed toward him. He kicked at the Sluggos, but more and more came.

The admiral raised his voice and announced to anyone left on deck who might be able to hear him, "I want to thank you all for your service. Your lives will not be lost in vain."

As the Sluggos swarmed over him, Haldane reached behind his head and hit the transfer pendant embedded at the base of his skull. His escape hatch.

He was going to miss this body, which had served him well for the past six weeks, but he gave little thought to the volunteer seaman who would transfer with him at the last moment.

If Admiral Haldane timed it right, the volunteer would feel only a few seconds of pain as the Sluggos devoured him.

It was what the volunteer had signed up for: He was just cannon fodder, and he had played the odds. Haldane couldn't even remember his name. Now it was time for the man to do his duty so that the valuable, experienced naval admiral could live to fight another day.

Haldane felt the alien jaws rip into his flesh. The pain was horrific, and he was glad to be out of that body.

2

When Paulson Kenz picked up his mail, he expected to find bills, junk mailers, delinquent notices on his student loan, even another eviction threat because his low-paying job didn't earn him enough to pay the rent and eat both in the same week.

The urgent draft notice, however, was far worse than any stack of bills or legal notices.

Paulson stared at the official envelope for a long time. Some of his friends in equally dire financial straits had talked about joining the military, but in the same distant way that they might talk about travelling to the Moon or signing up for a stint at one of the asteroid colonies.

Paulson knew he wasn't military material by any stretch of the imagination. A recruitment officer should take one look at his scrawny figure and muscles that could at best be described as "bookish," and laugh out loud before telling him to find a job as an accountant or librarian.

But libraries weren't hiring these days, and Paulson had no aptitude for accounting. With the increasing attacks by the alien Sluggos, however, the Earth Planetary Navy wasn't so picky.

His dismissive parents always told Paulson he was going nowhere, and now he had arrived—at nowhere. But now, as he held the EPN summons in his hand, he felt a chill. He would much rather be going nowhere than going into the planetary navy. Only the most desperate of military forces would take a bottom-of-the-barrel recruit like him, and if the EPN was that desperate then the human race was in dire straits indeed.

Retreating into his small apartment, he thought about calling his friends or his parents, but he didn't think his voice was stable enough for conversation. The draft notice allowed for no appeal. He needed to think about this, but the more Paulson considered his fate, the more terrified he became. He had been aware of the horrific alien invaders that attacked helpless vessels in the Pacific, but since he lived in a farming city in the Midwest, with little local industry, automated agriculture, nothing to attract tourists and very few job prospects, Paulson hadn't paid much attention to the Sluggos.

The notice commanded him to report to the training facility at the La Diego Naval Yards within three days.

The draft summons was legally binding and intimidating. The fine print said that any prior employment or contractual obligations were henceforth superseded. Payments and debts would be put on hold until the end of his EPN service.

Paulson read pages of instructions, a list of what to pack, and a helpful pamphlet on ways to prepare for this "exciting new phase" of his life. He fixated on a paragraph that advised him in the strongest possible terms to prepare a detailed Last Will and Testament before departing for the training facility. "Don't leave your family and loved ones with estate entanglements. Do the last brave thing in the event that you are unable to return home. A sailor in the Earth Planetary Navy must be prepared."

"I'll be prepared to die at sea," Paulson muttered. He didn't even know how to swim, but he supposed that wouldn't matter. If he fell overboard into a sea roiling with voracious Sluggos, treading water wasn't going to be much help.

Sitting alone in his apartment, glad that he had managed to get the power turned back on, he activated his entertainment and information screens to watch the news, which suddenly seemed relevant to him. A terrible nautical engagement and complete defeat had just occurred five hundred miles off the coast of Hawaii. Paulson felt physically ill as he saw the frantic jittery footage of creatures that seemed to be equal parts teeth and slime. The Sluggos swarmed across the deck of the destroyer that had engaged the alien infestation. Crewmen snarling, yelling in pain, sprays of blood, a tentacle the size of a redwood tree crashing down onto the *Far Horizon*, collapsing the bridge deck and communication mast and cutting off the transmission.

On the report, a tall young man with haunted-looking eyes wore a pristine white officer's uniform, his chest bedecked with so many medals and decorations that he had trouble standing up straight. He stood at a podium addressing hundreds of uniformed sailors who stood at attention. Hundreds of media reporters directed their imagers in the officer's direction.

"I am Admiral Bruce Haldane," he said, "and I recently

survived the *Far Horizon* engagement. I've faced the Sluggos three times now, and I've watched them destroy brave sailors, wreck civilian ships as well as military vessels. I am convinced there can be no negotiating with these creatures."

Paulson thought he seemed arrogant.

"With my experience and insights, I promise to do my best to develop an effective strategy to defeat these alien monsters. No more sailors need to shed blood into the sea. I am humbled by the sacrifice of all those who died on the *Far Horizon,* as well as the volunteer who formerly inhabited this body." Haldane touched his own shoulders and chest, as if to reassure himself of where and who he was. "That man gave his life so I could stand before you today and vow my revenge against the alien. Thanks to him, I can lead the EPN's retaliatory strike and wipe out those squirming bastards once and for all!"

Admiral Haldane raised a fist, but his movements were jerky and uncertain, as if he hadn't quite adjusted to his new body. It seemed to fit him like a stiff pair of new boots.

The crowd cheered regardless, and the media imagers captured the drawn and determined expressions on the sailors' faces as they vowed to avenge their fallen comrades.

Looking at the crowd of EPN seamen, Paulson could not picture himself as one of them, no matter what the draft notice said. He felt as if he had swallowed a hand grenade, and it was still in his stomach, ticking down the last few seconds. He couldn't run, couldn't escape the summons. He was DNA imprinted, and he had been chosen by a flawed lottery system: no exceptions. And he certainly couldn't argue that he was too valuable in civilian life.

He liked to read and ponder, but had never found the ambition to acquire a philosophy degree (which, in itself would not have led to a lucrative career). He was healthy enough, but only due to biological good fortune; he wasn't overweight, thanks to a natural metabolism. But he was sweating now, as if he had just run a marathon. Paulson didn't have many loose ends to tie up in his life, because he didn't have much of a life.

He had to figure out some way to get to the La Diego base. Because budgets were tight and all finances had to be devoted to constructing new Navy warships and weapons against the Sluggos, Paulson Kenz had to pay his own way to the last place on Earth he wanted to go.

THE NAVAL TRAINING center was aswarm with new recruits, herded about by junior officers as if they were a separated mass of Sluggos in human form. The chatter of conversation in the giant intake hangar was deafening; announcements over loudspeakers were garbled and incomprehensible. The background noise seemed to increase each time important instructions were given. Paulson expected this routine would have been more organized under normal times, but the EPN was undergoing quite an upheaval as they increased their ranks tenfold in response to the invasion.

Paulson stood among other recruits, some of them shiny-eyed and eager, jabbering with nervous enthusiasm. They pounded one another on the back, laughing and trying to outdo any braggadocio from their comrades. Paulson knew about such attitudes: patriotic young men and women ready to go off and kick some enemy butt. Most often that didn't turn out as planned. Some came home in body bags, others were lost forever. And the ones that did return were haunted for the rest of their lives.

Oddly, with so many disorganized people and so much chaos, the bureaucratic machinery hummed smoothly. Everyone flashed ID access cards and passed through human inventory kiosks into gigantic hangars where lines queued up, snaking around pedestals. Personnel Specialists studied each person that flowed into the larger base.

Paulson was confused and anxious, but he followed the person ahead of him, and he listened to instructions. When yeoman ran a quick gaze over him, studied his ID chip, then sent him into corpsman scan lines, he cooperated. He tried to keep his expression meek (which wasn't difficult at all). The intake officers studied the records displayed on their screens, narrowed their eyes, and frowned at him, then directed Paulson into a different line. Each time he met with more skepticism, was directed into a smaller line. He could tell he was being winnowed out.

They took blood samples and urine samples; they breathalyzed him; they performed a digital rectal examination, then a dental examination (mercifully changing gloves in between). They fitted a mesh hood around his scalp and took a brain scan. They gave him vision test, and then they clucked at all the results.

One nurse who looked as if she had retired from a Valkyrie squad loomed over him, knitting her eyebrows together. She turned to the yeoman at her side and spoke loudly enough to be sure Paulson heard her, "I thought we hit the bottom of the barrel last week."

"Sorry," Paulson said. "If you'd like to excuse me from service, I'll understand."

The Valkyrie-nurse gave him such an intense glare that his scrotal sac shriveled to the size of a prune, even though he had already been thoroughly checked for hernias.

"No one's excused," she said. "If nothing else, you'll do as cannon fodder."

3

Day by day, Admiral Bruce Haldane was growing accustomed to the new body, and he certainly had no time to waste. Fortunately, the volunteer had kept himself in good shape. The body was adequate, with a good frame, well-toned muscles. He was even handsome, in a way. Haldane was growing accustomed to what he saw in the mirror. Instead of being startled, he took the time to study his features, the dark hair, heavy eyebrows, the boyish expression of an innocent young recruit who had seen little horror in his life. But Haldane's eyes looked out from the face, and *he* had seen enough of war in the last few months.

Previously, his career had been soft and dull, but the Sluggos changed all that.

The volunteer's name had been Aaron Shelty, a seaman-apprentice who seemed a perfectly reasonable recruit for the Earth Planetary Navy, but he must have been a coward, because he refused to sign up for actual combat duty. *Too many people have grown as soft as the Sluggos*, Haldane thought.

After the mind transfer, Haldane had glanced through Shelty's dossier, looking at his grades, his performance in basic training. Everything seemed normal. Haldane couldn't understand why the man would sign up as cannon fodder. Shelty had left behind a fiancée, but she was young and pretty; she would find someone else before long. Shelty had parents and a sister, and they would all receive a compassionate and carefully-worded letter thanking them for Mr. Shelty's sacrifice aboard the *Far Horizon*. Haldane certainly appreciated the gesture, otherwise he would have died aboard the destroyer rather than his replacement.

It must have seemed like a good bargain when young Shelty had signed up for the program. The young man had gambled—whether through laziness or cowardice Haldane didn't know—that nothing would happen to Admiral Haldane. And the gamble had backfired on Shelty.

But Haldane benefited, and therefore the EPN benefited, and therefore the human race benefited. The admiral was alive, and he still had his expertise. The Earth Navy could count on him.

Yes, he was glad for Aaron Shelty's sacrifice, but was that sacrifice any more dramatic or extraordinary than that of all those seamen who had died, devoured or crushed under the onslaught of the alien slugs? Haldane didn't think so. Every person needed to do his or her duty, and Haldane needed to do his, even if it meant he had to swap bodies at the last minute and let the old body die on the battlefield. The war depended on him, and so it was worth the hassle.

Haldane looked in the mirror again, ran his fingers through the dark hair, made different expressions as he practiced the movement of his facial muscles. Yes, this body would do. Maybe he'd even pay a visit to Shelty's pretty fiancée. Now wouldn't *that* be a surprise!

But he didn't have time for that. There was a war on. After all the alien creatures were wiped out, however . . .

Unless something terrible happened again to him on the battlefield.

This time, the shock of the body transfer hadn't been as dramatic as when his original body was killed, when he'd been forced in that awful last second of indecision to push the transfer button on the implanted pendant, to give up his actual physical form, the one that had emerged from his mother's womb, the one he'd lived with all his life. But during the explosions, the firefight, and the horrific swarming Sluggos, after watching so many uniformed men and women torn to pieces around him, the decision hadn't been so difficult after all.

New body, same old job. He was back at EPN Headquarters in the La Diego main base, briefing world leaders, requesting new ships, more armaments, more depth pulsers, and an expanded fleet to attack the Sluggos.

As he drove in that morning, two Marines had tried to stop him at the outer gate. Though he had a new ID, the system had not updated his fingerprints, photographs, and DNA scans. Haldane made three increasingly angry calls until revised credentials were transmitted back to the guard shack.

After the *Far Horizon* tragedy, he had delivered his grand speech in this new body. Didn't they recognize him? Everyone on Earth should have seen the images of how the destroyer had been torn apart and sunk, all hands lost. How could these Marines not recognize Admiral Haldane's new body? He hated to be reminded that he wasn't as famous as he believed himself to be. Earth itself was under attack! Why wasn't every human being glued to their media and entertainment screens? Didn't they know that the fate of their planet was at stake?

After the fiasco at the guard shack, he finally made it to his office. As he entered, he still met the questioning stares, the double-takes from his staff as they tried to readjust to his new appearance. The Admiral's uniform had been altered, but the rank insignia and name plate were transferred over, same as before. Haldane was still himself, with his demeanor, his facial expressions. They would have to get used to it.

He sat behind his large desk and called up the day's intel reports of aerial flyovers and deep-water scans. His chief of staff, Ms. Tenn, entered the office and stood before his desk, running her eyes up and down his face and uniform. "I have your calendar, sir. If there's anything you need, please let me know."

"I need concentration time to reassess these images. Is there full documentation regarding new intel on the Sluggos? I need to plan our next strategy. There's some piece missing, and because I have the most experience, I'm the one to find it."

"It's all here, sir." Tenn leaned over the desk to activate Haldane's screen, calling up the messages he needed and spreading them out so he could sort and review them in whatever order he chose.

She brought him his usual bitter black coffee, but when he took a sip, it tasted strange. "Are you using a different blend, Lieutenant? Or does the brewer need cleaning?"

"No, Admiral. Same as always."

"Taste it."

He pushed the cup toward her, and she dutifully took a sip. "Tastes awful, sir, just like always."

Haldane shook his head. "Must be these new taste buds. Bring me a variety of coffees, lattes, cappuccinos, espressos. I need to sample them until I find one that tastes right on Aaron Shelty's tongue. Can't do my work without caffeine."

"Certainly, Admiral." She departed.

Haldane took another gulp of the bitter brew, struggled to swallow it, then pushed the cup away. That wouldn't do at all, and the inconvenience was troublesome. He'd have to compile a more detailed dossier about the next volunteer waiting in the wings. Shelty had passed all the required tests and his brain scan had been a match for Haldane's, but no one had thought to ask about his favorite foods or drinks. The admiral made a note of that.

On the screen, he called up the new messages. The Sluggos were damned difficult to locate under the water, but they were such a huge mass, millions of them writhing together, spreading out, moving a gigantic school of fish. Each time sonar bursts tried to pinpoint the location of the main mass, the swarm faded away and reappeared elsewhere. As soon as the mass of Sluggos was spotted, attack aircraft would drop explosives, which would kill a lot of fish and individual Sluggos—thus the military scientists had plenty of specimens, but very few answers. Even after the most horrendous explosions, though, the main Sluggo body would reappear and continue to attack.

All the EPN efforts thus far had only pissed off the squirming invaders, but Haldane wasn't going to use that as an excuse to relent. Even ineffective explosions were far superior —from a PR standpoint if nothing else—than letting the Sluggos do whatever they liked. The aliens had not proven to be good neighbors.

As humans expanded into the solar system, no one found any evidence of ancient Martian races or prehistoric Venusians, no Selenites under the craters of the Moon, no civilizations under the ice sheets of Europa, no bizarre creatures drifting among the asteroids.

No one knew where the Sluggos came from. Their ships were detected at the edge of the solar system by bored teams of asteroid mappers, but no one noticed their speed or incoming trajectory until the invaders had almost reached Earth orbit. Though the human military scrambled, the metallic teardrop ships hammered into the atmosphere like shotgun pellets and plunged into the Pacific Ocean.

Ships were dispatched to the area to see if they could find wreckage of the alien vessels, while news pundits demanded rescue efforts. Subs and diving bells went down to the crashed ships to save the benevolent alien visitors before they drowned. (Even then, Admiral Haldane knew it was a brash notion to assume that any alien visitor would breathe air instead of water.)

Considering the size of the alien ships, they should have been easy to find even in the deep water, but sonar detected nothing. The vessels seemed to have vaporized on impact.

The first attack struck a far-ranging Japanese whaler, the *Dragon Pearl*. The terrified crew transmitted images and distress signals, wailing for help as squirming conglomerate tentacles rose out of the water to smash the decks. After the initial horror subsided, Haldane thought that the scenes reminded him of a clip from a bad low-budget Japanese giant monster movie, some horrific rubber behemoth rising from the sea to toss about a toy model of a boat.

But the destruction of the *Dragon Pearl* was real, the

Sluggos were real, and the alien mass had attacked other cargo ships, an oil tanker (causing great consternation among environmentalists who insisted that the resultant spill was a greater threat to Earth than the alien invasion), and even a large cruise ship—all passengers and crew slaughtered on formal night. Recovered surveillance cameras showed frantic, swanky passengers trying to flee in their fancy tuxedos or slinky cocktail gowns and high heels.

Admiral Haldane had led the first unsuccessful responses against the aliens, embarrassed because he couldn't even find the Sluggos. When he finally did locate the enemy, they had destroyed his ship, killed his crew, and forced him to evacuate into a different body.

But he was the first one to notice that the Sluggos were pulling some equipment down into the water after destroying the ships, as if they meant to use the components, metals, antennae, even some of the weapons pieces.

The *Far Horizon* had been the Earth Planetary Navy's most heavily armed destroyer, and that too had been utterly destroyed, but Haldane did not feel defeated. He was back again in a new body, and he would continue to fight— although if he continued to die during engagements against the enemy, it would look bad on his record.

Ms. Tenn returned carrying a tray with seven cups of various coffee drinks. "I brought you a variety of options, sir. One of these should do."

"Thank you, Lieutenant," he said, then had a horrible thought. "God, I hope Shelty wasn't a tea drinker." He decided to be methodical about his testing. He closed all the records displayed on his screen. He would review them later.

Haldane fingered the implanted pendant at the base of his

skull. Sooner or later he would go out on another brutal engagement. He couldn't put this off. "Ms. Tenn, I want you to go through recruiting records so we can prepare for the worst-case scenario. This body is certainly adequate, but there's no telling what might happen to me. Find me a new volunteer."

4

———

Boot camp was hell—and Paulson meant that literally, as well as figuratively. (Yes, he did know the proper usage of the term.)

Throughout his life, Paulson was always the last person picked for any team sports activity. He played a good game of archaic chess, but no one considered that a "sport," despite his protestations. Any activity that required coordination, speed, strength or other physical prowess was not his forte. He had done a good job as a statistician, however. When he suggested that he be considered for such a role in the EPN, the training officer simply scowled at Paulson as if he were a form of nematode even lower than the Sluggos.

Because the alien invasion was now of immediate relevance to him, Paulson wanted to spend every spare minute scouring information about the alien invaders infesting Earth's oceans, but that plan quickly went out the porthole. All day long, the training officer tortured the recruits, forced them to do appalling exercises, tested their endurance. He did his best to kill every single trainee through exhaustion, screaming muscles, and cardiac failure before they had a chance to confront their first Sluggo.

Paulson struggled to memorize the rank system of the Earth Planetary Navy—no, EPN called it a *rating* system, just to make it more confusing, he supposed. He struggled to understand who outranked (or was it outrated?) whom. As a practical matter, it made no difference, since as a seaman-recruit, Paulson Kenz was lower than absolutely everyone. Even among the trainees who had been inducted on the same day, Paulson's performance set him apart—and beneath them all.

Inside the gigantic hangars, the recruits marched in ranks, drilling like robots, following nonsensical orders—moving back and forth, side to side, and around in circles, as if that sort of regimented pageantry would impress the alien hordes.

Paulson was in the lowest pay grade, but had no opportunity to spend what he earned. He was too sore, too exhausted and too miserable to read in the evenings. He felt nauseated, so he couldn't even eat the ill-seasoned chow they fed recruits. It seemed a sort of irony—perhaps intentional, perhaps a coincidence—that they had to eat seafood for every meal. Paulson plunged a fork into his fish sticks with a vengeance, as attacking a surrogate Sluggo.

His fellow recruits sat together, growling as they watched footage of the carnivorous slug creatures massacring Earth Navy ships. Some of the pale recruits whimpered in terror and recorded desperate messages for their sweethearts, but Paulson was simply too weary, wrung-out, and broken. He didn't know how he would get through another day.

If he ever did face a mass of Sluggos, he would be too bruised, battered, and weary even to lift a sidearm.

The next day was worse, and so was the day after that. The training officer was trying to toughen them up. The recruits practiced in the shooting range, trying to bull's-eye holographic Sluggos and receiving points for each kill. Paulson proved to be a poor marksman in every respect, although his score improved when they gave him scattershot guns. Paulson fired so many pellets in so many directions that he couldn't help but hit some of the aliens.

"You're lucky," the training officer said. "If the Sluggos attack, there'll be so many of them even you'll be able to cause some damage."

Paulson shuddered. Yes, that made him feel very lucky indeed.

Some of the recruits called the storm tank *fun*—the psychopathic recruits, as far as Paulson was concerned. The training tank simulated a storm-swept sea, cold churning waves complete with whitecaps. The recruits were thrown into the tank and told to struggle their way to a rescue buoy. Once they reached the buoy, they had to key in a safety code and solve some sort of puzzle before they could be retrieved from the freezing water and blowing winds.

Paulson could barely keep himself above the surface, flailing his hands, going under, inhaling water and then coughing it up. Simulated rain splashed his face so he couldn't see, but he felt stinging ice crystals. He shivered uncontrollably. He kicked his feet and tried to swim, but his sodden uniform was heavy and dragged him down. He could make out the other sailors reaching the rescue buoy, completing their tasks, and being yanked out by hover slings. Paulson couldn't do it, though. He went under, struggled back to the surface for a deep breath, and saw that he was drifting farther from the buoy. Even if he made it, he certainly couldn't remember the safety code. At the moment, he couldn't even remember his name.

He drowned during the exercise, one of three failures in the group.

But they revived him, and Paulson rolled over onto his hands and knees, retching onto the deck. He was still wet, freezing, miserable. All his muscles ached. His mouth tasted like vomit and seawater.

The training officer stood there, arms crossed over his chest, shaking his head. "Even a turd knows how to float. You're dumber than a turd. A complete and utter disgrace."

Paulson wasn't going to argue. He sucked a lungful of air and croaked, "I wouldn't want to do anything halfway, Sarge. Glad I'm not only a partial disgrace."

The training officer was not amused. On his pad he called up Paulson's records, then frowned to spot a fresh set of urgent high-priority orders.

"I'm just not cut out to be a seaman, sir," Paulson said.

The training officer roared, "Don't call me 'sir'! You don't deserve to call me 'sir,' turd!"

"Sorry," Paulson said. "It's all so confusing."

The training officer turned the pad around, showing Paulson's brain scan and a high-priority request from Admiral Bruce Haldane himself. "You see that, turd? You're a match—for better or worse, though I don't know why the Admiral would accept someone like you. I can't force this decision on you, but I can offer to transfer you."

"I . . . I don't know what you're talking about."

"Of course you don't, turd. You don't need to know. But here's something you actually *can* do—I suggest you take it."

WHEN HE MET ADMIRAL HALDANE, Paulson recognized the man who had delivered the speech honoring the sacrifice of those who had lost their lives on the *Far Horizon*. In earlier media glimpses, Paulson had also seen images of Admiral Haldane's previous incarnation. This new version seemed younger, taller, less salty, but the hard expression was the same, as was the swagger of his movements . . . and of course the nameplate on his chest beneath all the medals.

Haldane did not seem to be impressed. "You're the volunteer."

"Seaman-recruit Paulson Kenz, sir." He saluted, then hesitated, considered his words, and realized that 'sir' was indeed appropriate in this circumstance.

"You realize what you're being asked to do, seaman?"

"No, sir. No one's briefed me at all."

Haldane shot a glare at his chief of staff, a female officer who stood looking as prim as a mannequin in a department store window. "Sorry, Admiral, he must have slipped through the cracks. Seaman Kenz, you are being offered a chance to be Admiral Haldane's next alternate-in-waiting. We would like to install an interchange conduit at the base of your skull, which is linked to an identical one in the Admiral's head."

Haldane turned, showed Paulson the implanted disc at the base of his skull.

"The Admiral has a great deal of direct experience and innate knowledge about our enemy, about the tactics used by and against them. Such knowledge cannot be lost, nor can it be replaced. Therefore, the Earth Planetary Navy has developed extraordinary measures to preserve that brain trust—and you will help us do it."

"You mean, I'm going to become cannon fodder?" Paulson said.

"That is an inaccurate term," Haldane said. "The Sluggos don't use cannons."

"Why would I want to do that?" Paulson asked. "If you get in trouble, then I'll die, right?"

"That's a big 'if,' seaman. Until recently, I lived my entire life without dying, and I've learned a great deal with each successive engagement against the enemy. I believe we come closer to finding the key to their ultimate defeat with each encounter."

"In the meantime," Tenn interrupted, "you will be excused from any dangerous duty, any further training, any military drills. You'll have a comfortable existence. You'll be given quarters, food, and very few responsibilities. It's a cushy job, Seaman Kenz. You wait to be called up, and hope you won't be. If you agree to be the Admiral's alternate-in-waiting, then that will be your only duty for the duration of your contracted service."

Haldane seemed annoyed at the situation. "In other words, you just sit around and read or play games, although you're expected to keep yourself in shape." He raised his arms, flexed his muscles. "The previous owner of this body did a good job, and we'll count on the same from you. Are you willing to take the gamble? You're my escape hatch so I can live to fight another day." He paused, added a greater threat to his tone. "Your other alternative is to go back to boot camp and be put on the next ship, where you'll face an engagement of the Sluggos. In person."

Paulson swallowed hard. He'd seen the images of the *Far Horizon* massacre, listened to the howling crew, saw the chomping teeth of the Sluggos. He had watched how the aliens moved in eerie concert, forming a gigantic organism that was far more ferocious than the sum of its parts.

The decision wasn't hard for him.

"I accept, sir. It's a gamble, but it's really my only option. If I get out there facing those things as *me*, I know I won't survive." Paulson fingered the back of his head, felt the smooth hardness of his skull. He supposed the surgery was going to hurt. "I'll take my chances with you."

5

It came from beneath the sea.

The next time the mass of Sluggos appeared, they did not prey upon Navy ships patrolling the open seas; rather, the new conglomerate monster rose up out of Pearl Harbor and attacked land for the first time.

Tour boats and naval patrol ships spotted the incoming surge, but no one understood what was happening at first. Hundreds of thousands of Sluggos swam in individually like the world's entire population of eels meeting in Hawaii for a convention. The arm-length creatures glided in under the surface, choking the channels, filling the harbor.

Tourist boats were buffeted by the swarms of soft shapes with sharp teeth. Naval destroyers, missile cruisers, fast frigates, and even a huge old battleship were brought to bear. General Quarters sounded and the crew raced to their stations. The dockyards were put on high alert.

The squirming worm-like things choked the harbor, but that was just a start. The Sluggo bodies coalesced, braiding together, building up like pieces in a gigantic wriggly mosaic sculpture—until a huge and hideous monster rose out of the sea.

Rushing down to the harbor from his satellite headquarters office, Admiral Haldane screamed for fishing boats and salvage cutters to string nets that would stop the numerous individual Sluggos from joining one another, but it was too late. The things became a gigantic mound of squirming flesh, as if a mad artist had made a nightmare sculpture out of living maggots. The Sluggo mass extruded pseudopods and began smashing any vessel in the harbor.

Admiral Haldane had been sent to Oahu, not for a tropical vacation but to organize the EPN Pacific Fleet's plan to dispatch numerous search-and-destroy subs that would find the Sluggos. Unfortunately, the alien monsters decided to be found right there on the Earth Navy's doorstep.

Pearl Harbor was full of Navy ships, tourist boats, and cargo barges hauling goods in lightweight crates for launch at the Honolulu Spaceport. Like a child playing with toys in a bathtub, the conglomerate Sluggo monster crawled over vessels and pushed them under the water, crushing their hulls and sinking them. Other pseudopods snatched desirable equipment and whisked it away beneath the surface.

Admiral Haldane dispatched fighter jets loaded with missiles. As the giant monster hulked its way on top of the floating museum battleships and onto shore, the roaring jets launched missiles that blasted the huge monster, dispersing it into countless squirming Sluggos that sprayed in all directions. But the monstrous mass shuffled and reorganized itself somewhere else, heading toward the rocket launch area of the spaceport.

Haldane didn't like this one bit. "Let's try napalm. We must have some left over."

Tenn called up summaries on her datapad. "None of the new formula is weaponized yet, sir, but there may be some old leftovers in storage."

"Never let anything go to waste," Haldane said. "We might as well use it up."

"There's plenty of fuel spilled on the water from all those damaged ships, sir. Igniting that could be effective as well."

"Good idea. Let's do both."

The EPN battleships launched huge sprays of missile, and the sky became a messy finger-painting of smoke, mostly from damaged structures, exploding naval ships, even one crashed jet when the Sluggo-beast had thrashed a unexpectedly whip-thin and unexpectedly long tentacle into the air to snatch and crush the plane, before hurling it onto the deck of a snorkeling cruise boat just being loaded with a senior citizens' tour group.

The Sluggos moved like an enormous blob, rising up to capsize cutters. Large-caliber artillery guns hammered away at the mass, destroying thousands of individual Sluggos, but the overall monster did not seem affected.

"Open the weapons lockers," Haldane yelled. "Distribute weapons to anyone who won't turn and run. Rifles, shrapnel pulsers, pea-shooters—I don't care."

"We may have a shortage of pea-shooters sir," Tenn said.

"That was a joke, Lieutenant."

"Very funny, sir."

Haldane thought this might be a war of attrition: humanity just needed to kill off enough of the individual Sluggos, which were easily destroyed. But the supply of squirming aliens seemed inexhaustible.

Out in the harbor, a group of sailors were making a last stand with rifles and hand grenades. No one could understand how all those little maggot things could work together to create a single massive and apparently intelligent organism. They kept tearing apart ships, stealing components. Haldane knew the aliens had built starships that had carried them to Earth from some other solar system.

But how did these silly little worms know what to do when they were linked together? A million humans certainly couldn't cooperate like that. Often it was hard to get three people to agree.

More light bombers roared overhead, dropping explosives, including cannisters of old napalm. The intensely hot flames from the jellied gasoline crisped the outer layers of squirming worms. They blackened and fell away, but new Sluggos boiled up to take their places. More and more Sluggos streamed into the harbor from the open sea, adding themselves to the monster's bulky conglomerate body. Even after so many individual aliens were destroyed, the overall bulk swelled.

The pseudopods extended outward, moving the mass away from the naval ships to the reserved spaceport area. The Sluggos snatched tall gantries and pulled rocket shuttles and girder structures down off the launch pads. The squirming creatures dragged those components into the water of the harbor.

Haldane shouted orders because he was expected to, but no one could hear him in the deafening noise. The oddest part was that the giant alien monster moved in silence. It simply created havoc without adding any extraterrestrial commentary.

Haldane considered calling in a nuclear strike. Oahu was

beautiful, but there were other islands in the Pacific. And if it took such an extreme measure to get rid of the Sluggos once and for all, despite the loss of the entire population, including himself.

He had grown fond of his new body from Aaron Shelty and didn't want to use the escape hatch too soon, especially now that he had seen the alternative-in-waiting, the scrawny slip of a man named Paulson Kenz. But Haldane couldn't think of himself at a time like this.

The tentacles broke the keel of an aircraft carrier that had entered the harbor, and that was enough to force Haldane's decision. He was really getting upset now. Yes, he had to call in a nuclear strike for the good of humanity.

Before he could issue the order, though, a slimy tentacle burst out of the water right at the shore's edge and swept all of them aside, including Admiral Haldane. He found himself flying through the air, flailing. Another series of explosions roared nearby.

He shouldn't have waited! He grabbed for the back of his head, trying to find the transfer pendant. Others were sailing through the air near him, screaming, bloody, broken.

There! He found the pendant. Emergency transfer with the volunteer—

But then Haldane slammed into the side of a boat house, splintering the shingles. The pain was brief, the unconsciousness swift.

This time, he doubted he would live to fight another day...

.

He awoke in the medevac hovercopter along with a dozen other broken and bleeding casualties. Haldane felt as if someone had made kindling of his ribs and spine. A corpsman hunched over him, poking and prodding until he got the proper response to his question of "Does that hurt?" Other doctors tended the wounded.

"I see by your insignia that you're a admiral," said the corpsman.

"I am, dammit!" As much blood came out as words. He could tell this was bad. He tried to lift his hands, but his arms were strapped down. "Help me. I'm Admiral Bruce Haldane. I need to activate my exchange pendant."

"Sorry, sir, I can't let you move. There could be internal damage."

Haldane was appalled. The corpsman didn't understand what was going on here. "I don't care about my injuries! Before I die, I need to transfer." He began coughing again and felt the warm blood on his lips.

"Good news for you, then, sir—you're not going to die. Just rest easy. You suffered some broken ribs, a shattered clavicle, probably a severe concussion. But our deep scans show no obvious internal bleeding. We just want to be careful."

"So I'm going to . . . recover?" Haldane said. That shouldn't have been disappointing.

"Looks like it. We'll patch you up." The corpsman looked shell-shocked; his expression was gray. "You're one of the lucky ones. Over fifty percent fatality rate from the monster attack. They'll be a long time counting up the casualties. I think . . ." He shook his head. ". . . I think Pearl Harbor is gone. Half of Honolulu is gone. Fires are raging. The Sluggos sank most of our fleet, destroyed the spaceport, then they withdrew."

"Is there any good news?" Haldane asked.

"I just told it to you. The Sluggos departed, slithering back into the ocean. That's the best news you'll hear."

"Oh."

"That, and the fact that you're going to live. Should be enough good news for the day, right, sir?"

The corpsman shot him full of sedative. As he sank down, Admiral Haldane knew he would be a long time healing, which was upsetting. Thankfully he could keep this body, even though it was going to hurt like hell when he woke up. At least he wouldn't be a 90-pound weakling.

6

Even with the tension that was always in the back of Paulson's mind, his daily duties here—as in, no useful duties whatsoever, only busy work so the EPN could feel confident in their investment—certainly beat basic training. Instead of being aboard a ship hunting for voracious alien monsters, his duty station was a giant rec room.

The surgery to install the transfer pendant was as unpleasant as he'd feared: having a hole drilled in the back of his head, a sensor plug and transmitter installed with a million self-seeking wires plunging into his brain, where it found the core of personality and memories. The exchange conduit would tear out, record, and transmit everything that was Paulson Kenz, then re-upload the very being of Admiral Bruce Haldane—in the event that circumstances warranted it. Paulson kept his fingers crossed and hoped.

Paulson had healed up after the quick coagulant slather, and the pain meds had been nice until they ran out (budget cuts, with all the best stuff reserved for any EPN soldiers wounded in combat).

There were fifteen other volunteers inside the guarded recreation hall. They were forced to remain in the La Diego base, but it wasn't so bad. All fifteen of them had the exchange conduit installed in their heads, tethered to other command officers or political leaders that were deemed too valuable to lose.

Two volunteers played ping-pong, but neither was very good at it. One man, who had already put on fifteen pounds, placed orders from the galley and ate all day long. Paulson knew the food was not at all tasty, but at least the quantity was comforting. Just this afternoon, though, a dietician had come in, take control over the man's eating habits, and advise (as well as enforce) nutritious meals. "You are required to take care of your body," the dietician said in a decidedly threatening voice, "in case it should be needed."

The volunteers seemed to have a free ride, but they were obligated to take care of themselves. Although *they*, as individuals, weren't important, their bodies were considered vital to planetary defense, and the Navy had made a considerable investment in them. Some volunteers took the task seriously and worked out in the fitness center, lifting weights, jogging on the treadmill. Paulson did the required calisthenics, but he had never seen the purpose in picking up heavy things and putting them back down again, or running on a piece of equipment that went nowhere.

He remembered how his parents had told him <u>he</u> was going nowhere, that he spent too much time reading, paying little attention to practical things. They had been right, according to their own definitions. Now, they were probably proud of him for being a part of the brave Earth Planetary Navy. If he were called upon to provide the mortal escape hatch for Admiral Haldane, they would be pleased as punch to tell their neighbors about how their good-for-nothing son had become a war hero.

Paulson didn't feel particularly brave. Any heroic end on his part would be completely out of his hands. Most of his fellow volunteers had resigned themselves to an imminent and unpleasant demise, grabbing as much life as they could in the meantime, playing games, horsing around, sleeping in. Several had written up a petition demanding access to a military-approved escort service, and that request was currently working its way up the chain of command.

Paulson was the only one who cared about the war against the Sluggos, and about increasing his chances for survival, as well as the rest of humanity's, in a worst-case scenario. Because he was cerebrally paired with Admiral Haldane, he requested access to the briefings on the invasion and records of prior Sluggo attacks, in hopes of teasing out any vulnerabilities. He studied news reports, although the most detailed, and most gruesome, footage was missing.

He requested additional intel, including the full classified reports, but since he was just a seaman-recruit, with the lowest possible security clearance, his request was summarily denied. So, he submitted an appeal, documenting that he was the functional physical equivalent of Admiral Haldane, that his body—and therefore the structure of his brain—would be used by the leader of the Earth Planetary Navy. Therefore any information might be beneficial, should the admiral be forced to swap bodies with him. Paulson also pointed out that if the admiral ever did activate the transfer protocol, Paulson himself would be rapidly devoured by aliens, and therefore all secrets would be safe.

The yeoman, who was harried and overworked, didn't entirely understand the nuances of the argument, but rather than risk annoying the real Admiral Haldane, he bumped the request up the chain. Somehow, it got approved. Accidentally, Paulson supposed.

In the rec hall/prison, he spent hours poring over the records, watching the movements of the Sluggos through the water during the rare times they were tracked. But whenever sonar rigs tried to track the large conglomeration, the entire mass vanished like a puff of smoke. Maybe they just dissociated into a million little worms again, invisible to sonar traces.

The EPN knew about where the alien invaders lived beneath the Pacific, a broad general area where their starships must have landed. Supposedly, that was where their base might be.

He studied biological reports of the creatures. Many Sluggo specimens had been dissected, individual nematode-like things that had very little physical structure. Each Sluggo was just a sac with a few rudimentary organs, a digestive system, and a mouth with sharp teeth, but no eyes or other obvious sensory apparatus, not even a brain, just a small nerve cluster.

It made no sense that these things could combine into some gigantic entity that obviously had a structure and a purpose, and was presumably intelligent. The Sluggos used tools, they built machinery, constructed spacecraft, and flew interstellar distances. Not bad for a bunch of hungry worms.

In the specimen tanks or dissection trays, they didn't look any more sophisticated than extraterrestrial leeches. When

Sluggos moved en masse in the water, they looked like a gigantic school of fish, somehow moving with one mind. He shook his head.

Then the pendant at the base of his skull began to tingle.

The rec hall around him fuzzed. The ringing in his ears grew as loud as church bells, and he wavered. Other volunteers in the rec hall looked up, sensing something amiss.

"It's happening!"

This was too soon! He wasn't ready. No one had even told him Admiral Haldane was going out to fight with the Sluggos. It would have been nice to have a little more warning.

He felt as if his soul were rushing down a wind tunnel. He left his body, yelling—but without making any sound.

And when he woke up he was somewhere else, inside a different body. And he screamed in agony. He felt shattered bones, torn muscles, a bashed head, nerves that clamored about all the bodily damage. He tried to open his eyes, but he was surrounded by white blurs, moving faces. Doctors? If he was going to die, he wished he could at least stomp on one or two Sluggos first.

Then the pain was too much, and he faded into unconsciousness.

HE AWOKE to find his own face staring down at him.

Paulson recognized himself, saw the body at the bedside —*am I really that scrawny?*—but realized that the eyes were different. Then the pain hit him again, so he wished he hadn't woken up. The agony was somewhat diminished from before, and he was a little foggier. He could feel painkillers like slimy wet velvet working through his mind and body, but he could also feel the physical damage. He knew this body was mangled.

This wasn't his body in the first place . . . so many things didn't feel right. Meanwhile, Paulson watched his own body pacing back and forth in the infirmary room, studying the medical equipment and monitors that provided a discordant symphony of bleeps. His own face turned toward him, and in all his life of looking at himself in a mirror, he had never seen his expression show such disapproval before.

And his reflected image had never talked back to him, either. "Good to see that you're awake. I need to explain the situation, and then be off to a briefing." His voice sounded funny.

Paulson croaked in a rough voice, "You're not dead." This had to be Admiral Haldane. The vocal cords weren't his own, and the tone sounded wrong in his head. His throat was sore —he must have been yelling or screaming before the swap.

"I was badly injured during the battle of Pearl Harbor. I thought I was a goner there for awhile, and I almost used the transfer during the worst part, but I got walloped before I had the chance."

Paulson's body shrugged. Admiral Haldane touched his new shoulders, felt the bones there, encircled his wrist with thumb and forefinger. He clucked. "You really need to take better care of yourself, Kenz. Put on a few pounds, preferably muscle."

"I'll leave that up to you now, sir," Paulson said.

"This transfer is just temporary while that body heals," Haldane retorted. "The doctors said I was going to live, but the recovery would be hard and painful. I don't have time for that bullshit—there's a war on. And then I thought, what do I have *you* for? Now, you just lie there and heal. It's the least you can do in service to your country and your planet."

Haldane leaned over the infirmary bed and prodded the bandages in Paulson's side. Paulson gasped, nearly fainted from the rush of pain that exploded through him. Haldane continued. "A few broken ribs, lots of bruises, stitches in a half dozen places. Oh, and they removed your spleen, but you can do without that. When was the last time you used your spleen?"

"Never noticed it before, sir," Paulson said, trying to be stoic.

"The medics are pumping you full of accelerated cell growth. Your body's got so many bruises all over that your skin has natural camouflage. But that'll heal. The bones will heal. The physical therapy is going to be rough, but you can handle it. I don't have time—I have meetings."

Paulson lay back and just felt the aches piled upon aches. He had dreaded being called upon to transfer with the admiral, but this, he supposed, was the best realistic scenario. He was still alive. He could lie here and recover in the admiral's place, as he asked.

And whenever the fuzzy painkillers wore off, maybe the EPN would even provide him with a reading library so he could catch up on some of the books he'd meant to read.

"Be quick about it healing," Admiral Haldane said, before turning around. "I'll want that body back again as soon as you've fixed it."

7

———

Something about the scrawny body of Paulson Kenz inspired disrespect despite the medals and rank insignia on the uniform. Kenz was bookish, shy, the sort of person who simply begged to have beach sand kicked in his face by a bully of even modest proportions.

The more days Admiral Haldane lived inside the other body, the more he noticed the subtle attitude shifts toward him.

When the admiral entered the La Diego base headquarters, he carried his revised ID and temporary access cards, with Paulson's fingerprints and retina map transferred over to his diagnostics records. It was just a temporary situation, though, since he expected to swap back to his preferred body as soon as the damaged one was healed in sick bay.

Previously, Admiral Haldane's very presence had inspired instant deference, but in Paulson's body he had to work at it. As he marched down the passageway, a pair of junior officers strolled by, engrossed in conversation and paying little attention to him. Annoyed, Haldane placed himself directly in their path so that they were forced to look up and notice his insignia and name badge. They scrambled to give the proper salute accompanied by hasty apologies.

Haldane walked on, not entirely satisfied. War was all about sacrifices, he supposed. He could endure this one.

It wasn't just the fact that he felt physically weak, that he grew winded after climbing only five flights of stairs, that simple acts such as opening a pickle jar or carrying a box of classified printouts to the shredder were more difficult. He didn't like the way he looked when he took a shower, couldn't imagine suavely trying to pick up a woman in a bar or, even more embarrassing, taking her home where he would have to make bedroom excuses: "This isn't really my natural body. My normal endowment is much more impressive." He could already imagine the seen-it-all-before looks of skepticism. . . .

He was still trying to get his office in order, breaking in a new chief of staff, since his adjutant Ms. Tenn had been inconveniently killed during the Sluggo attack on Pearl Harbor. Her death had caused innumerable problems.

In his office, the interim replacement had brought him the morning coffee, a cinnamon cappuccino, which, after thorough testing, was what Haldane and Ms. Tenn had determined best suited his Aaron Shelty taste buds. He gave a grunt of thanks and sipped the coffee as he sat down—but it tasted awful. He had forgotten. Paulson Kenz's body preferred something else entirely. Haldane growled in his throat and drank the cinnamon cappuccino anyway, forcing it down because he simply didn't want to bother to get it done right.

He had work to do and a world to save.

The morning's reports made the day seem much brighter.

He studied the new images and grinned, then he immediately called together his highest-level advisors.

THE BRIEFING ROOM was full of high-ranking EPN officers, prominent politicians, and even businessmen in charge of massive amounts of funding—all the important people who could make the proper decisions without the delay of red tape. The secure conference room felt like a cave; the original design had been to evoke the comfortable camaraderie of an exclusive gentlemen's club.

"Gentlemen," Haldane said, before nodding toward the lone female in the room, "and ma'am. We have wonderful and fascinating intelligence—our reconnaissance has finally borne fruit!" In his ears, Kenz's voice sounded squeaky.

The lights in the briefing room dimmed further as he displayed images on the wall screens.

"With the attack on Pearl Harbor, the Sluggos showed their real intent. They are going to infest our oceans, then swallow up our islands, then devour our coastlines. Who knows, they may even chew canals wide enough to bring them all the way to Kansas. And as you well know—" He narrowed his eyes and swept his gaze across them. "—we have no naval bases in Kansas."

He saw the determined faces around the room nodding gravely. An unnamed man in a business suit folded his hands and leaned forward. "You've already convinced us, Admiral. No one disputes the magnitude of the alien threat. Our ship-yards and weapons factories, our naval construction operations have been blossoming like weeds. Just tell us what you *can* do, and we'll give you everything you need."

Haldane smiled. Throughout his EPN career, his ideas had been met with reluctance and resistance, thanks to narrow-minded individuals and the web of red tape they spun. Now, Admiral Haldane had everything he could possibly ask for. All he had to do was ask. Even in his scrawny body, these advisors looked to him, respected him, understood the weight of experience and wisdom he brought to these discussions.

Among the inner circle gathered here, he knew that at least six of them had transfer circuits implanted, because they were deemed to be powerful and influential enough to be classed as irreplaceable. They had their own escape hatch volunteers.

"I have faced the Sluggos several times in person, at the cost of two previous bodies and damage to a third. I've looked them in the eyes . . . well, at least in the slimy membranes. I have watched men and women die all around me, and I've felt myself die. I know what it's like. I was aboard the *Far Horizon* until its last moments. I was there at Pearl Harbor. And I'll be there again at our final engagement."

He changed the images on the screens to show blurry sonar readings. "After the attack on Hawaii, the Sluggos withdrew with many vital spaceport components, dragging them beneath the sea. We've been trying to find their secret base. A fleet of fast mapping survey ships cruised over the surface, covering thousands of square miles of open sea. They were ready to map every inch of the damned Pacific if they needed to. And this is what they found."

He zoomed in. The sonar trace showed the gigantic mass of Sluggos that had formed the conglomerate monster. The echo was bigger than a hundred giant squids as it moved along the ocean floor. The first image of the huge alien mass was sharp, the second was fuzzed and blurry.

"With the third sonar ping," Haldane continued, "the Sluggo mass had vanished—as usual. But this time it's different, because we found where those creatures go to bed."

The sonar trace showed the ocean floor, a low-resolution image that nevertheless revealed a city of permanent undersea structures, a hodgepodge assembled from wreckage the creatures had stolen.

"Knowing where to look, we dropped off submersible microcameras, self-guiding imagers that dove down to the coordinates. They were small enough to remain unnoticed— for a time."

Haldane displayed crisp video feeds as the submersible cameras dove to where the invaders had built their submerged fortress. At such a depth, the water was dark and murky; activating bright lights to penetrate the gloom, the microcameras revealed bizarre free-form sculptures, towers and domes that were welded together with mud and coral. The structures incorporated the wreckage of ship hulls, including the bridge tower of the *Far Horizon*, along with sunken wrecks dragged hundreds of miles from Oahu.

The buildings themselves, however, seemed to *squirm*. As the microcameras flitted closer, they revealed that the walls were also built out of Sluggos. The worm-like creatures piled up like soft flexible bricks, many of them dead, others dissolving and oozing into organic cement. Gantry structures stolen from the Honolulu spaceport served as frameworks, and individual Sluggos crawled up the girders, wrapping around them like putty.

"Unfortunately, the lights the cameras used to obtain these images attracted attention," Haldane said.

The images on the conference room screens switched to static one at a time. The last microcamera zoomed in on one of the eel-like creatures swimming toward it, its mouth gaping wide until it swallowed the camera, which valiantly transmitted a last few images of the alien digestive sac until the acid destroyed it.

Haldane crossed his arms over the many medals on his now-scrawny chest. "So there you have it, gentlemen." He nodded to the woman again. "And ma'am. We pinpointed their base. We know where they're lurking." It felt good to grin. "We have a large expeditionary sub being converted into a battle vessel. It was originally designed to complete a full sonar map of the ocean floor, but now we have more important work for it."

The man in the business suit nodded. "Ah, the *Prospector*. We funded that. One of our subsidiaries is developing domed underwater housing as condo time-shares, and we were going to lay claim to all that undeveloped real estate. We're having trouble selling shares, thanks to the Sluggo infestation."

Haldane nodded. "We know sonar does little good to track them, but we can arm the *Prospector* to the teeth. It's got a reinforced hull and expanded magazines to accommodate more than fifty torpedoes. I'll find a determined crew. We'll be ready to make our final assault within a week. I intend to lead the expedition myself and blow the living slime out of those Sluggos!" He smiled. "If I have your permission."

They gave him their exuberant approval, but the lone woman asked, "Why wait a week if we know where the Sluggos are now?"

"It'll take that long to get ready, ma'am. We have to give this our best shot."

Admiral Haldane had an ulterior motive. In a week, the infirmary would release his other body. Paulson Kenz had finished the basic healing process, and he was completing the final physical therapy schedules.

If he was going to defeat the alien invaders once and for all, Haldane certainly didn't want to be wearing this scrawny body for the history books.

8

After all the snide comments and complaints Admiral Haldane had made about Paulson's original weakling form, the young seaman-recruit wished the admiral had been more careful with this one. If Haldane hadn't let himself get so smashed up or killed—twice in fact—then Paulson wouldn't have to spend his days here in the infirmary being tortured by a Spanish Inquisition of physical therapists who used enhanced healing therapies and supercharged hormones that pummeled his muscles and bones until they knitted themselves together—or else.

The physical therapists had a bedside manner more appropriate for the Marquis de Sade than Florence Nightingale, and Paulson was very quickly convinced that he wanted to be released from their clutches as soon as possible. He longed to be back in the rec room hall again with nothing to do except study reports on the Sluggos.

Even here in sick bay, however, as soon as he grew strong enough, Paulson called up all available images of the

Honolulu attack. Because so many vacationers spent time in Hawaii, most of the footage had been confiscated from home-made tourist videos. Paulson watched the rampaging conglomerate monster that had destroyed the ships in the harbor, the spaceport, the buildings on the shoreline.

He was more interested in poring over clips taken prior to the assembly of the Sluggo monster. He watched how the myriad organisms drew together like some kind of group mind, how the individual worm-things assembled into a much larger and adaptable body that reorganized itself according to circumstances. The Sluggo organism was clearly intelligent en masse, though the individual creatures showed only the most rudimentary brain activity. After the harbor attack and ransacking the ships and spaceport, some of the retreating Sluggos had maintained enough physical integrity to haul off the wreckage they desired, while the rest of the creatures dissolved like a mist of maggots.

Even if sonar couldn't track the massed alien organism underwater, fast ships could have followed the sunken ships and the spaceport gantries as the Sluggos hauled them away. But with Pearl Harbor, the EPN base, the waterfront, and the spaceport destroyed, no one managed to think that far ahead.

Paulson walked on a treadmill, limbering up his legs. He still felt lingering broken-glass pain in his ribs and shoulder. His numerous bruises had turned an alarming bouquet of colors, but the flesh tone was returning. The therapists often studied his body, finding patterns and designs in the discolorations. One even exclaimed that he saw the face of the Virgin Mary there. Paulson thought he was joking, but the man's voice held no sarcasm or humor whatsoever.

During the treadmill work, he sweated heavily and his

pulse raced. He was ready to drop, but the therapists egged him on and threatened him. Paulson was surprised they enhance his sessions with a bullwhip just to keep him moving. After weeks of physical therapy, he began to long for the days of boot camp, which had been miserable enough, but at least he'd been able to sleep at night.

On the other hand, if he hadn't signed on to the escape hatch program, he would have been doomed to go out and fight the alien monsters. He probably would be a statistic from Pearl Harbor. In most ways, being dead was worse than physical therapy.

According to the doctors' estimates, given additional enhanced jolts of healing chemicals, in a few days he would swap back into his own body and return to the rec hall with all the other transfer volunteers. And wait.

Admiral Haldane appeared in the therapy center just as Paulson stumbled off the treadmill and the therapists yanked the monitor electrodes from his scalp and chest.

The admiral regarded him with obvious impatience.

"Hurry up and finish healing, Seaman Kenz. The clock is ticking, and I want that body back. I'm due to head into battle again, and I'd rather face the Sluggos wearing that—" He jabbed a finger toward Paulson's borrowed body. "—than this."

"Healing as fast as I can, sir."

"He'll be ready on time Admiral," said the physical therapist who had seen the Virgin Mary in his bruise patterns. "I'll give him a double maximum dose tonight."

Haldane seemed to consider Paulson as little more than a piece of equipment; he paid attention to the medical specialists instead. "And have you scheduled the cranial reset surgery yet?" He tapped the pendant on the back of his head—Paulson's own head—and glanced at Paulson, who stood panting and sweating beside the treadmill.

"Cranial surgery again, sir?" Paulson said. "I didn't agree to that."

"Yes, you did," Haldane said. "It's in the fine print. The transfer conduit is set for one-way transmission only, one-time use. It has to be that way, if you think about it. After I evacuate from a critical last-stand situation, I can't have my volunteer just hit the pendant again and reset."

Paulson ran his fingers along the small disc on the back of his head. "So now that we've transferred, we can't just switch back?"

"We'll just pop out the device and put in another one," said one of the medical techs. "Easy as replacing an eyeball. Piece of cake."

"You'll be happy to get your own body back, Seaman Kenz," said Haldane, "and I'll certainly be glad to have that one. We located the main undersea base where the Sluggos are building their fortress, and I'll be taking an expeditionary sub there rigged as a battleship with plenty of megatorpedoes and missiles. It'll be glorious!"

Paulson decided it was time to share what he had gleaned from his research on the aliens. "Sir, I've been studying the enemy behavior. The Sluggos seem to be a group organism, collectively intelligent but individually not much. The Sluggos are just like cells, bound together by some kind of telepathy. They cooperate, bond with synergy, and—"

"Yes, yes, very nice, Seaman Kenz," said Haldane. "With all the megatorps loaded aboard the *Prospector*, we'll blow the Sluggos to hell and level their undersea base. The ruins will be the next best tourist attraction since Atlantis."

9

———

They didn't have time for a proper commissioning cruise aboard the *Prospector*. The crew would get accustomed to their battle sub, and he would get reacquainted with this body, by the time they reached the coordinates of the sunken alien base.

Admiral Haldane touched the sore spot in the back of his skull where the transfer conduit had been replaced. His freshly healed body still ached; he could feel the lingering remnants of bruises, and his bones twinged when he moved the wrong way. Nevertheless, it felt good to be out of that weakling form. These aches and pains were a good sort of hurt, like after a heavy workout. In the body of Paulson Kenz, his tired soreness just felt like hopeless surrender.

In the week since the discovery of the alien undersea base, the Sluggos had remained quiet, though aircraft and high-resolution satellites made several tentacle sightings.

Admiral Haldane was the EPN's highest-ranking officer and he insisted on commanding this mission, but he had never served aboard a sub before, so he let the actual captain, XO, navigator, and weapons officer do their jobs without interference. Normally, a admiral with Haldane's clout and experience would never have been risked on such a dangerous mission—and at least half the *Prospector*'s crew was convinced this would be a one-way trip. Admiral Haldane, though, intended to face the squirming enemy one last time. He wanted to see them all splattered into plankton-sized pieces.

The *Prospector* needed his background and experience during what was sure to be intense fighting. He knew the sub's crew might panic at the wrong moment, so he had to lead them with his proven abilities. Besides, he always had his escape hatch.

During the long and tedious voyage, Haldane spent much of his time on the bridge, watching the screens. The navigator sent sonar bursts, but the waters remained clear. He called for numerous drills and targeting simulations, loading and unloading torpedoes. The admiral also worked out in the sub's makeshift exercise area, limbering his restored body and working through the last aches and pains.

When the *Prospector* reached the coordinates of the Sluggo base, the sub, the crew and Admiral Haldane's body were ready for action.

"We'll strike fast, and repeatedly," he said over the horn from the command deck, glancing over at the captain and XO. "Like ninjas. One megatorp after another after another. You all saw the size of that monster that attacked Pearl Harbor. I'd say twenty megatorps should be sufficient, and that leaves thirty more to obliterate the base." He waited for the resounding cheer, then glanced at the captain. "Captain, prepare your firing pattern."

The captain snapped, "Weps, Fire Control, you have your orders."

When they approached the target, the sonar technicians sent out pings to map the alien structures ahead. For an instant he saw a shadow of the monstrous conglomerate creature, but it disappeared by the time of the second burst.

In the blurred sonar images, he saw the huge alien structures, which seemed significantly larger than what the microcameras had recorded a week ago. Some of the towers appeared to be falling, the domes collapsing.

"That sonar resolution really sucks," he said.

"We're close enough that we can see with our own eyes, Admiral," said the XO. "Lighting it up now."

Haldane smiled with pride at the efficient crew. "Captain, I'll turn operations over to you. Handle all the details, please."

The sub's brilliant lights stabbed into the deep, dark water, illuminating the bizarre alien fortress. Around them, the water was aswarm with millions of the squirming eels, but the gigantic conglomerate monster was not in sight. The dismantled ship hulls and spaceport gantries stood on the sea floor— and they were slowly toppling down. The base seemed to be falling apart by itself.

Everyone stared at the startling images, momentarily frozen. Haldane roared, "What are you waiting for? Fire control, launch megatorps!"

The crew had been tense and waiting, with hair-trigger fingers. The first megatorpedoes soared out like javelins on a tail of foam. The weapons crew was already loading the second volley even before the first had hit.

Haldane muttered to himself, "This is going to be good."

The torpedoes arrowed straight on target and struck the

Sluggo base with glorious detonations. Haldane caught his breath as bright shock waves blossomed like an explosive cluster of flowers. The sonar techs switched off their ears before the close-range blasts rang out, and thunder reverberated through the *Prospector*'s hull. Haldane was caught off guard, but the rest of the crew hunkered down at their stations. Fire control shouted a succession of orders.

As admiral, he wanted to be in control and direct all activity, but the others reacted so quickly without him, like a well-oiled machine. Within seconds, another volley of megatorps was away. This would be a constant punishing brawl, and the squirming aliens didn't have a chance.

Explosions wrecked the undersea structures. The broken hulls and gantry frameworks were already toppling, but then he saw a flurry, as if the megatorps had startled a flock of carrion birds. Individual Sluggos boiled up from the patchwork structures by the thousands—tens of thousands.

Haldane realized that all those huddled invertebrates had been *holding the base together*, like living building blocks. Sluggos had covered the scrap components, but the explosions had stirred up all those creatures, which now abandoned the structures and swarmed toward the sub like angry hornets from hundreds of disturbed nests.

Contradictory orders echoed throughout the *Prospector*. Haldane intended to give some kind of brilliant insight that would allow the crew to make a wise and instantaneous response, but the best he could vocalize was "Uh-oh. Keep firing megatorps."

The weapons officer yelled, and the crew aft in the torpedo room kept frantically loaded volley after volley into the launch tubes like a fire brigade. Explosions hammered the crumbling alien base, but the uncertain and scattered cloud of free-swimming Sluggos simply swirled around. Then the swarm came toward the sub like an angry school of fish.

"Keep firing!" Haldane yelled, as if the crew needed any encouragement.

Countless writhing shapes formed a cloud that congealed around the *Prospector*. The squirming bodies in the swarm wove together, fastening one body to another, and another conglomerate alien creature formed itself like a giant fist around the battle sub.

The last three megatorps launched, but became caught in the thick amorphous mass. The detonations were like sledge hammers pounding the *Prospector*'s hull, and throwing the crew to the deck. Haldane lost his balance and slammed into a control station, knocking the sonar tech aside. He climbed to his feet, shaking his head. On the main screens, they saw all the water go dark as the mass closed in.

"All megatorps gone, sir," said the captain. He looked sickened.

"Already? This is not possible!" Haldane said. "Fifty megatorps struck their targets! We destroyed the alien base!"

Nobody argued with him. The fire control and weapons officers knew the explosions had caused damage, but the huge squirming mass of Sluggos just reformed into a giant and powerful mass of angry flesh.

The *Prospector* groaned and shrieked as even the reinforced armor was bent beyond its tolerances. The intercom was filled with shouts.

"Watertight doors closing! Breach on Deck Five!" the XO yelled.

The battle sub lurched, and the deck tilted at an angle. The huge alien creature had grabbed the hull and was squeezing and shaking the *Prospector* as if it were nothing more than a toy.

"Another hull breach on Deck Three, Admiral," the XO yelled. "Water's coming in."

"And so are the Sluggos!"

The Prospector's captain gave him a beseeching look. "You've faced the Sluggos before, sir. In your experience, how should we fight off this thing? We need you to tell us."

Haldane didn't know, but he was aware that he had to escape. The sub would collapse any minute, and someone had to return with a full report to the main EPN base. Humanity would count on him to debrief his fellow admirals. With each engagement, Admiral Haldane learned more and more, and now he had to tell someone that even megatorps didn't work.

"Even failed missions can be instructive," he said, making sure he sounded brave. "But we have to keep fighting until the last possible second. Full ahead. Can we use our engines? Maybe we can break free of this slimy mass."

The captain gave the order while shaking his head. The engineer yelled through the horn. "The Sluggos are caught in the propellers, This vessel is frozen and shut down, and our reactor's at 110%. Any more of an overload and it's going to go critical—fifteen minutes, max."

Haldane thought fifteen minutes sounded highly optimistic. "If the reactor goes critical, maybe that'll take out these things. We all have to be brave right now." Their bravery, of course, would manifest differently from his own.

"Sluggos inside the sub!" yelled someone from the torpedo room. "They broke the hatches, pushed their way through the tubes! We're taking on water—water and Sluggos. Compartment's filling up!"

Haldane wanted more details, but the torpedo officer spent too much time screaming and so wasn't very helpful. More damage reports came from other decks. "Thousands of Sluggos are aboard!"

Haldane thought of the wriggling forms, slithering along the decks like carnivorous maggots, attacking anything that moved. The *Prospector*'s hull groaned and lurched again. The captain and XO looked at each other, expressions white.

Haldane was amazed at how swiftly the invading Sluggos reached the command deck. He had faced these awful things before, had seen the horde wipe out Pearl Harbor, and seen them take down the *Far Horizon*, had felt them squirming over his body and sinking fangs into his flesh in the seconds before he activated the escape hatch transfer.

Knowing there was nothing to do and no point in delaying, Haldane faced the bridge crew. This was their last stand. They were out of weapons; alien invaders had breached the hull. Without question, the *Prospector* was doomed.

Haldane accepted the inevitable. Although he wasn't looking forward to escaping into the scrawny body of seaman-recruit Paulson Kenz, he knew that even a weakling form was better than a dead one.

"Thank you for your service and bravery, crewmen. Your deaths will not be in vain. I shall deliver the story of your brave final battle, your last stand for humanity."

The weapons officer gaped at him. "You're just bugging out!"

The XO glowered. "He's saving his own skin."

Haldane lifted his chin. "I'm living to fight another day. It's the only way Earth will defeat these monsters."

Twenty of the squirming, sharp-fanged Sluggos lurched onto the bridge, and several crewmen yelled in terror. Haldane touched the transfer pendant in the base of his skull.

As reality faded around him, he was indeed proud of the *Prospector*'s crew. He saw their faces . . . but for some reason, they didn't seem particularly glad to know that he, at least, would survive.

10

When Paulson Kenz felt the wrenching inside his head and found himself whisked back into Admiral Haldane's surrogate body, he knew the poop had hit the fan—industrial-sized cargo load of poop.

Struggling with disorientation, he found himself was on the command deck of the battle sub that had gone to attack the Sluggo undersea base. It was a shocking transition from his comfortable padded chair in the rec hall, where he'd been studying reports of the mission, looking at the parameters of the *Prospector*.

He had gone over the list of added weapons, the reinforced hull, the fifty megatorpedoes loaded aboard. From what he suspected about the alien biology, Paulson was skeptical that explosive kinetic weapons would solve the problem at all. But Admiral Haldane had not demonstrated much ability to think outside the box.

He would assume he had enough firepower to level the alien base, then return to cheers and parades. The problem was, blasting the Sluggo monster to pieces wouldn't help, because it was already in pieces. The alien swarm was fundamentally composed of countless individual units bound together by some kind of common telepathy.

Admiral Haldane had not been interested in hearing any suggestions from a scrawny piece of cannon fodder, though.

Knowing the sub intended to engage the invaders' base, Paulson had watched the meager intel as it came in, preparing himself for the worst, since the admiral's previous engagements had not turned out well—especially not for the "escape hatch" volunteers. The waiting was maddening.

The other volunteers in the rec room amused themselves by playing ping-pong or engaging in interactive games. None of them bothered to become friends, sure that any one of them could be called to duty and dispatched at any time.

Paulson could feel them looking at him with pity. Admiral Haldane's track record, and his recklessness (which Haldane tried to characterize as bravery), was no secret. Right now, he was leading his battle sub to the monstrous horde. Paulson hoped for the best, but he didn't get his wish.

This time, when the conduit in his head activated, he knew exactly what was going on—and he was ready.

He braced himself during the transition, and when he gazed out through a different set of eyes, this time he wasn't in a safe sick bay, nor was he being evac'd from a battlefield.

Instead, he saw several slithering, eel-like creatures with round hungry-mouths and white diamond-like teeth. They squirmed forward along the deck, bursting onto the bridge, or command deck, or whatever it was called on a submarine. The alarms were deafening, as were the shouts of the *Prospector*'s crew. Uniformed men and women made their last stand and fought the Sluggos, stomping and hammering, using any possible weapon. The sub's captain had a handgun and shot into the soft masses, and they exploded like snot-filled water balloons. Some bullets whanged and ricocheted off the bulkheads, making the other crewmen duck.

Through the main port, Paulson saw only a solid writhing mass of interlinked Sluggo bodies, as if someone had placed the worm aliens into a trash compactor and smashed them up against the *Prospector*.

Paulson only had a second to assess the situation. More Sluggos slid through the hatch onto the bridge; twenty were already making their way to the controls. Two bloodied seamen threw themselves against the bulkhead door, ramming their shoulders and pushing the heavy metal hatch into its jamb, slicing two Sluggos in half.

The captain, the XO, the weapons officer, the fire-control officer, the sonar tech—all of them were completely disregarding Paulson. He had an idea, but he needed their help, and their attention. "Captain, give me a situation report," he barked, surprised at the sound of his own voice.

The startled captain turned to look at him. "You're not the admiral—you're just cannon fodder."

"We're all cannon fodder, but I'm wearing the uniform. I've got the rank, I have the authority . . . and I have an idea. What's our weapons situation? Tell me what's happened and where we are."

"We're up a creek without a paddle," the XO cried. "Megatorps gone, and our hull is completely engulfed by Sluggos. At least four hull breaches, and the aliens are swarming through all the decks."

The engineering officer wiped sweat from her forehead.

"Structural failure imminent, sir. Catastrophic hull collapse in three minutes." Her voice was hoarse. "Or less."

"I predicted the megatorpedoes would be ineffective," he said.

"I wish you'd been in the Admiral's body before we got in this mess, then," the captain said.

Paulson didn't want to argue. "Do we still have sonar?"

The sonar tech climbed back to his feet, held onto the anchored chair. "Sonar didn't do any good, sir."

Paulson believed they'd been misinterpreting the results. The Sluggo monster didn't know how to become invisible to the sonar pings; rather, the massive organism had actually *broken apart* and then reacoalesced.

"I want a sonar burst, the loudest boom you can make, Mr. Lieutenant—Ensign . . . sorry, I don't know your rank."

"My rate," said the sonar tech.

"Does the sonar work or not?" Paulson snapped. From the design specs, he knew the *Prospector* had been built as a survey vessel, with a full complement of sonar mapping gear.

"We can send out a ping as loud as bad rap music coming from a car stereo."

"Then let's hope it sounds as annoying as that."

As the sonar tech scrambled with his controls, Paulson yelled to the communications officer, "Send a message throughout the ship . . . the sub, or whatever. Close all compartment doors, seal off the bulkheads. We need to separate the clusters of Sluggos." He had noticed that after the crew sealed the door to the bridge deck, the individual worm creatures were less lively, more disoriented, and without a driving goal. "We need to divide and conquer. The Sluggos are a conglomerate organism. If you separate the pieces, the pieces are no longer intelligent."

The sonar tech removed his ears. "Here we go." He activated a loud pulse that thrummed out. The response was immediate and startling.

The Sluggo mass surrounding the *Prospector* shivered and broke apart like flies taking flight from a pile of manure. At the main port, Paulson saw hundreds of the things peel off from where they'd been compacted against the view port, and they scattered away from the sub. Even the Sluggos inside the command deck were dazed from the sonar blast, which gave other crew enough time to stomp on them and pop their body sacs.

"Another ping! Keep it up!" Paulson shouted.

The tech stared wide-eyed at the controls. "Did you see that?"

Paulson ran over and grabbed him. "Keep pinging! The sonar disrupts whatever binds them together into a collective organism. It may be our only chance!"

The tech launched another loud boom, and most of the remaining Sluggos drifted away from the sub's hull like flakes of dandruff.

"I can keep pinging all day!" the tech yelled excitedly.

"You may have to do that. Call the engine room—see if that freed our propellers so we can get the heck out of here."

"They're called screws, sir," said the engineer.

The reactor room called up to the bridge. "We're free—and the reactor's running at peak. I'm going to burn off some of our excess by setting off at top speed."

While studying so many reports, Paulson had tried to determine what held the Sluggos together like a million brain cells in a single coordinated organism. Now he was grinning. "Keep hitting *them* with sonar blasts, and they won't give us any more trouble. Our pulses are scrambling the single intelligent creature into countless unintelligent cells. They won't be able to reassemble into anything big enough to threaten us."

Now that the main port was clear, Paulson could see the ocean around him. He saw the wreckage strewn on the sea floor, the components and debris the Sluggos had used it as a structural framework. The megatorps had indeed destroyed the base at least, but if the big structures were held together by conglomerated Sluggos, the aliens could just rebuild as soon as the individual worm-things settled down. By then, though, the *Prospector* would be far away. So long as the sonar pulses kept scrambling the Sluggo mass, the sub could move unimpeded.

Another sonar boom resounded through the water. The sea around them was a boiling swarm, but the scrambled creatures didn't attack the sub. Inside, the crew were rapidly dispatching the Sluggos one at a time.

"Blow all ballast," Paulson ordered in his loudest command voice, then turned to the captain and whispered, "That's the best way to get us to the surface, isn't it?"

The sub's captain turned to look at him with a dawning respect. "Indeed, Admiral. I'll take it from here, sir. You've already saved the day."

"You may have saved the human race," the XO added.

The captain ordered, "Put us on the ceiling!" He nodded at Paulson. "You might want to hold onto something."

Soon, the *Prospector* breached the surface like a humpback whale. It was a short but exciting ride, and for the first time

Paulson felt excited about being part of the Earth Planetary Navy. On the scope, the seas were peaceful and Sluggo-free.

"Our comm systems are damaged," the XO said. "Can't send anybody the good news until we make repairs."

"Then we have to get back to port and report," Paulson said, glad to be getting out of this with his skin intact. "We're going to live to fight another day."

11

From the main press podium at the La Diego Earth Navy base, Admiral Bruce Haldane wore his formal uniform again, the one that had been re-re-tailored to fit Paulson Kenz's scrawny body. It was his body now, a permanent swap now that the *Prospector* had been lost. But he could always upgrade. He had already sent out a call to the recruitment offices and among the current sailors. Thanks to the Sluggo threat, new recruits were being drafted by the tens of thousands, processed as quickly as was bureaucratically possible. Certainly, with so many choices available, there must be someone better qualified than this wet-noodle bookworm.

Still, the escape hatch had worked, and Haldane was relieved to be safe again. He vowed to carry on the fight for Earth. . . .

As soon as he had transferred out of his body aboard the battle sub, he found himself in the recreation hall along with the other lazy slobs who took the easy way out, all those young men who were too afraid to face down the voracious Sluggos as Haldane had done—several times.

Settling into the bookworm's body, he brushed himself off, glared at the rest of the volunteers, and marched to the guarded door, demanding to be taken to base headquarters. Medical monitors would have picked up the transfer signal, so they would come to investigate before long, but he needed to meet with the advisory board, issue his report, and add his new information to the growing backlog of data. Someday, his experiences might allow teams of human geniuses to discover some small weakness in the aliens.

And he also had to make his announcement, putting forth a brave face for the people of Earth.

At first, the guards didn't want to let him out of the rec-hall prison. They looked at Paulson's scrawny body and regarded him with skepticism.

"I am Admiral Haldane, I tell you! Let me loose, I have to make my report."

The guards raised their eyebrows. "Sure, you are. And you expect us to just release you without confirmation?"

"I'm *me*, dammit! That's all the confirmation you should need." Haldane realized that he would have to correct this flaw in the system.

One of the other volunteers looked up from a suspended game of ping-pong. "That one's been acting awfully strange. Could be an adverse reaction to the conduit surgery."

The others nodded. "I wouldn't believe him."

These cowardly slackers didn't respect him! "This is nonsense!" Haldane shouted at the guard. "I outrank you. I'm your admiral!"

"I heard him talking," said another volunteer. "He said he

was going to escape and find a black-market surgeon who would pop out a plug for a fee."

The lazy bastards were setting him up! Haldane was furious.

Finally, a signal from medical command informed the guards that Haldane's transfer protocol had been activated, and that the escape hatch swap had been successful. He gave an annoyed huff toward the slovenly volunteers who thought it was all a joke, then he stormed out. This was an emergency, not a minute to lose!

Ever since the *Prospector*'s launch, all of Earth was waiting to hear the news. They expected to learn that the invaders had been annihilated, their base destroyed, and any other Sluggos from the Sluggo planet would see that the Earth Planetary Navy was nohing to mess around with.

When he delivered his speech in his weakling body, though—not the one that had departed aboard the battle sub —he could see dismay ripple through the crowd. They'd already figured out that the mission had failed, that the Sluggos were still a threat . . . and they assumed that the *Prospector* had been lost with all hands. That much was obvious, because otherwise the admiral would never have used his last-ditch escape plan.

The captain of the submarine would have gone down with his ship, as expected, but a war hero like Bruce Haldane had survived to rouse the troops, to inspire the populace and honor the sacrifices of those who had fallen in battle, as well as to advise the EPN's tactical experts.

Standing at the podium, he activated the loudspeaker systems. His words pounded out across the gathered crowd. "You may not recognize me, but I am Admiral Bruce Haldane.

And I have just come from the embattled submarine *Prospector*. With fifty megatorpedoes, we wrought terrible damage to the alien base, but the Sluggo retaliation was swift and overwhelming. They engulfed the sub, and I . . . I regret the loss of all hands."

He cleared his throat. "A list of all names will be made available to you in subsequent press packets." He lifted his chin and kept his tone stoic. "However, even failures are instructive. We believed that a megatorp bombardment was our best possible hope, but now we'll just have to try something else. Maybe undersea nuclear saturation. It's worth a try."

He drew a breath. "Let us pause for a moment of silence to honor all those who sacrificed themselves aboard the *Prospector*." He closed his eyes, bowed his head—and then an actual signal from the *Prospector* spoiled the moment.

The excited announcement broke through on the loudspeakers. The media reporters were abuzz. The battle sub had survived after all, had surfaced intact and was now making its way at best speed back to land!

Admiral Haldane straightened his cap, squared his shoulders and forced a smile. "Oh . . . well, then. This is wonderful news."

12

———

An escort of EPN destroyers met the *Prospector* as it approached the La Diego harbor. People gathered on public docks to welcome the victorious vessel with remarkable fanfare. The cheers from the crowd were deafening.

When Admiral Haldane went to greet them as part of a formal reception party, he was all smiles and pride.

In the days it had taken the battle sub to return, the *Prospector*'s crew had become heroes. No further Sluggo attacks or even sightings had been reported. The sub's captain had transmitted that they had only escaped by using the "sonar defense suggestion" of "Admiral Kenz" to great success, and they believed they had found a way to eliminate the alien invaders once and for all.

"Admiral Kenz" indeed! Haldane fumed inwardly.

As the *Prospector* docked and Admiral Haldane stepped out to greet them, the captain and the XO disembarked with an altogether too smug looking seaman-recruit Paulson Kenz.

The sailors looked battered and bruised, their uniforms tattered. Haldane thought their disheveled appearance was strictly for dramatic effect, because even after the Sluggos had swarmed through the decks, the officers and crew must have had a clean change of clothes aboard.

Haldane said, "I'm so pleased you all made it." He waited for the sub's captain to salute, and the man did so, but reluctantly, keeping his eyes fixated on the Admiral's insignia rather than his face. "We welcome your return home, and we look forward to your report about the end of the engagement."

The XO blurted out, "Our report will include how you abandoned us, Admiral Haldane—how you took us into danger with reckless disregard for the lives of the *Prospector's* officers and crew."

Haldane was shocked. "I led an attack that had a reasonable probability of success, but it didn't work. Such are the fortunes of war."

"Excuse me," said the sub's captain, "but Admiral Kenz said he advised against your method from the outset, but you refused to listen to his advice."

"His *advice*?" Haldane spluttered. "*Admiral* Kenz? He's just a recruit, cannon fodder! I'm the real admiral!"

"As far as I'm concerned, you relinquished that title when you abandoned the ship and crew." The captain cleared his throat. "Sir."

"I was required to survive," Haldane said. "I waited until the last possible moment, when there was no hope for survival. I saw no other way."

"And yet . . ." The XO nodded at Paulson Kenz. "After you fled for your life, this untried seaman-recruit assessed the situation, solved the problem, saved all our lives, and defeated the

Sluggos—in about two minutes. I believe that's called a battle-field promotion, sir."

With a sinking sensation in his gut, Haldane realized that all of this was being recorded and transmitted live.

In the familiar strong and handsome body, Paulson Kenz said, "I've even worked out a way that we can use continuous sonar for complete victory. You see, each pulse scrambles the Sluggo hive mind, breaks it apart. If we bring in numerous subs and keep hammering them with sonar so that the individual creatures cannot re-coalesce, then we can use nets or tanks as a harvesting system. If we winnow down the individual Sluggos so that no more than a hundred or so can gather in any single place, the group intelligence won't come back. Divide and conquer. It may take time, but we can simply whittle them away until there are no more Sluggos left."

"Thank you for that interesting suggestion, recruit." Haldane put all the scorn he could possibly muster into his voice. "We'll have our experts take it under advisement. For now, it's best if we initiate the transfer protocol again, swap back so you can have your original body, and I'll make my announcements and appearances in—"

Paulson raised his head. "Sorry, sir, but as you informed me, it's a one-way transfer protocol. We'll have to reinstall and surgically reset the conduits, but there's no time to go through that now. I need to present my findings to all the command advisory board. There's a war on, you know."

The captain and the XO ignored Haldane and looked at Kenz. "What are your orders, Admiral?"

Paulson looked flustered. "Well, we need the submarine fixed up and cleaned, for one thing. Then we have to discuss how to implement my sonar strategy so we get rid of the Sluggos."

"I demand my body back!" Haldane said.

Paulson plucked at his sleeve. "I don't believe this is your original body any more than that one is. Meanwhile, you can spend time in the recreation hall with the other cannon fodder volunteers. You should have plenty of time to write a personal letter of sympathy to the families of each of those *seamen* who died during the attack on the *Prospector* . . . and on the *Far Horizon* . . . for starters."

"But you're just a . . . a nobody!" cried Haldane.

The sub's captain said, "We believe Admiral Kenz has valuable insights and irreplaceable knowledge and experience. The EPN could not afford to lose him, so he must be preserved at all costs."

"Yes," the XO added, "it would be a grave threat to the human race if Admiral Kenz were to be lost in combat. I'm sure the escape hatch conduits can be adjusted. You can wait with the other volunteers." He narrowed his eyes and gave Haldane a withering look. "Don't worry, you'll be called to do your duty, if needed."

PRISONER OF WAR

1

The first Enemy laser-lances blazed across the battlefield at an unknown time of day. No one paid attention to the hour during a firefight anyway. Neither Barto nor any of his squad-mates could see the sun or moon overhead: too much smoke and haze and blast debris filled the air, along with the smell of blood and burning.

A soldier had to be ready at any time or place. A soldier would fight until the fight was over. An endless Now filled their existence, a razor-edged flow of life-for-the-moment, and the slightest distraction or daydream could end the Now ... forever.

With a clatter of dusty armor and a hum of returned weapons-fire, the defenders charged forward, Barto among them. They had no terrain maps or battle plans, only unseen commanders bellowing instructions into their helmet earpieces.

Greasy fires guttered and smoked from explosions, but as long as a soldier could draw breath, the air always smelled sweet enough. Somehow, the flames still found organic material to burn, though only a few skeletal trees remained standing. The horizon was like broken, jagged teeth. No discernible structures remained, only blistered destruction and the endless bedlam of combat.

To a man who had known no other life, Barto found the landscape familiar and comforting.

"Down!" his point man Arviq screamed loudly enough so that Barto could hear it through the armored helmet. A bolt of white-hot energy seared the ground in front of them, turning the blasted soil into glass. The ricochet stitched a broken-windshield pattern of lethal cuts across the armored chest of one comrade five meters away.

The victim was in a different part of the squad; Barto knew him only by serial number instead of a more personal, chosen name. Now the man was a casualty of war; his serial number would be displayed in fine print on the memorial lists back at the crèche—for two days. And then it would be erased forever.

Barto and Arviq both dove to the bottom of the trench as more well-aimed laser-lances embroidered the ground and the slumping walls of the ditch. As he hunched over to shield himself, the helmet's speakers continued to pound commands: "KILL ... KILL ... KILL ..."

The Enemy assault ended with a brief hesitation, like an indrawn breath. The soldiers around Barto paused, regrouped, then scrambled to their feet, leaving the fallen comrade behind. Later, regardless of the battle's outcome, trained bloodhounds would retrieve the body parts and drag them back to HQ in their jaws. After the proper casualty statistics had been recorded, the KIA corpses would be efficiently incinerated.

In the middle of a firefight, Barto and Arviq could not be bothered by such things. They had been trained never to think of fallen comrades; it was beyond the purview of their mission. The voice in the helmet speakers changed, took on a different note: "RETALIATE ... RETALIATE ... RETALIATE ..."

With a howl and a roar enhanced by adrenaline injections from inside the armor suits, Barto and his squad moved as a unit. Programmed endorphins poured into their bloodstreams at the moment of battle frenzy, and they surged out of the trench. The Enemy encampment could not be far, and they silently swore to unleash a slaughter that would outmatch anything their opponents had ever done ... though this most recent attack was assuredly a response to their own previous day's offensive.

Moving as a unit, the squad clambered over debris, around craters, and out into the open. They ran beyond monofilament barricades that would slice the limb off an unwary soldier, then into a sonic minefield whose layout shone on the eye-visor screen inside each helmet.

With a self-assured gait across the no-man's-land, the soldiers moved like a pack of killer rats, laser-lances slung in their arms. They bellowed and snarled, pumping each other up. As he ran, Barto studied the sonic minefield grid in his visor, sidestepping instinctively.

From their embankment, the Enemy began to fire again. The smoky air became a lattice of deadly lines in all directions. Barto continued running. Beside him, Arviq pressed the stock of his weapon against his armored breastplate, pumping blast after blast toward the unseen Enemy.

Then a laser-lance seared close to Barto's helmet, blistering the top layer of semi-reflective silver. Static blasted across his eye visor, and he couldn't see. He made one false sidestep and yelled. He could no longer find the grid display, could no longer even see the actual ground.

Just as his foot came down in the wrong place, Arviq grabbed his arm and yanked him aside, using their combined momentum. The sonic mine exploded, vomiting debris and shrapnel with pounding sound waves that fractured the plates of Barto's armor, pulverizing the bones in his leg. But he fell out of the mine's focused kill radius and lay biting back the pain.

He propped himself up and ripped off his slagged helmet, blinking with naked eyes at the real sky. Arviq had saved his life—just as Barto would have done for his squad-mate had their situations been reversed.

Always trust your comrades. Your life is theirs. That was how it had always been.

And even if he did fall to Enemy attack, the bloodhounds would haul his body to HQ, and he would receive an appropriate military farewell before he returned to the earth—mission accomplished. A soldier's duty was to fight, and Barto had been performing that duty for all of his conscious life.

As he activated his rescue transmitter and fumbled for the medpak, the rest of the soldiers charged forward, leaving him behind. Arviq didn't even spare him a backward glance.

2

———

Some said the war had gone on forever—and since no one kept track of history anymore, the statement could not be proved false.

Barto knew only the military life. He had emerged from a tank in the soldiers' crèche with the programming wired into his brain, fully aware, fully grown, and knowing his assignment. If ever he had any questions or doubts, the command voices in his helmet would answer them.

Barto knew primarily that he had to kill the Enemy. He knew that he had to protect his comrades, that the squad was the sum of his existence. No good soldier could rest until every last Enemy had been eradicated, down to their feline spies, down to the bloodhounds that dragged away Enemy KIAs.

Winning this war might well take an eternity, but Barto was willing to fight for that long. Every moment of his life had encompassed either fighting, or learning new techniques to kill and to survive, or resting so that he could fight again the next day.

There was no time for anything else. There was no need for anything else.

Barto remembered when he'd been younger, not long out of the tank. His muscles were wiry, his body flexible without the stiffness of constant abuse. His skin had been smooth, free of the intaglio of scars from a thousand close dances with death. Barto and his squad-mates—apprentices all—had fought hand-to-hand in the crèche gymnasium, occasionally breaking each other's bones or knocking each other unconscious. None of them had yet earned their armor, their protection, or their weapons. They couldn't even call themselves soldiers....

Now consigned to the HQ infirmary and repair shop, as he drifted in a soup of pain and unconsciousness, Barto revisited the long-ago moment he had first grasped a specialized piece of equipment designed to maim and kill. The soldier trainees had learned early on in their drill that any object was a potential weapon—but this was a spear, a long rough bar of old steel with a sharpened point that gleamed white and silver in the unforgiving lights. A weapon, his own weapon.

He spun it around in his hand, feeling its weight—a deadly impaling device that could be used against the oncoming Enemy.

Later, his advanced training would of course include hand-to-hand combat against other soldiers, human opponents ... but not at first. All trainees were expendable, but if the young men could be salvaged, then the military programming services would turn them into killers.

For months, Barto received somatic instruction and physical drilling by one of the rare old veterans who had survived years of combat. The veteran had a wealth of experience and survival instincts that could not be matched even by the most sophisticated computers. He made sure that Barto fought to the limit of his abilities.

Swinging the spear against nothing, feeling his body move, Barto reacted to the barked commands of the veteran instructor. Response without thought. He learned how to make the weapon into a part of him, an extension of his reflexes. He was the weapon; the spear was just an augmentation.

Then they gave him a taste of blood, real blood. They wanted him to get in the habit of killing.

The small metal-walled arena was like an echo chamber, a large underground room with simulated rock outcroppings, a fallen tree, and other sharp obstacles. Barto didn't question the reality of the scenario. The environment itself was a tool to be used.

During that exercise, the veteran instructor let him wear his helmet ... but nothing else. Stripped naked, he gripped the spear in his hand and glared through the visor. The helmet earphones gave him reassuring commands in his ears, directions, suggestions. Otherwise, Barto felt helpless—but no soldier was ever helpless, because a helpless man could not become a soldier.

Underground, the arena door groaned open, and barricade bars moved away. Barto tensed. He gripped the metal shaft of the spear despite the sweat on his palms.

Suddenly, a whirlwind of bristles and scales, sharp hooves and long tusks launched itself like a projectile. An enhanced boar with scarlet eyes snarled and plowed forward, searching for a target, something against which to vent its anger.

And Barto was the only other creature in the room.

On high pedestals in the gallery above, three enhanced cats watched, blinking their gold-green eyes. The feline spy commanders observed for the invisible overlords who wanted to see how the freshly detanked soldiers reacted in their first real life-or-death test.

The boar charged. Barto jabbed with the spear, but he was too tentative. Before, he had only thrust at imaginary opponents and an occasional hologram projected inside his visor. Now, though, the boar came on like a locomotive. The spear glanced off, opening a mere stinging scratch in the creature's skin. Barto had not imagined its hide could be so tough, its bones so hard. He had made the first, terrible mistake in this duel.

The trivial wound enraged the beast.

Barto dove to one side over a synthetic rock, and the boar rammed into the artificial tree trunk. It spun around, shaking its head, tusks gleaming. The ivory spears in its mouth looked much more deadly than Barto's primitive weapon. The boar attacked again.

A moment of panic rose up like an illusion, but he pounded it back, and the fear evaporated, bringing a rush of adrenaline. The chemical and electronic components in his body released the substance, making Barto see red rage of his own.

The enhanced boar recovered itself and snorted. Barto knew he had a better chance of striking the target in motion if he didn't use a tiny pinpoint thrust; instead, he swung the heavy metal bar sideways like a cudgel. The sturdy steel bashed the creature's thick skull. The sound of the impact rang out in the hollow room.

The cats watched from their pedestals.

The boar squealed and thrashed. Barto saw that its eyes held an increased intelligence, like that found in the feline spies and in the daredevil bloodhounds that retrieved bodies from the battlefield. The boar responded with a calculated counterattack, trying to outthink this naked human opponent, this would-be soldier. Barto smiled; the boar was the Enemy.

In the frenzy of battle, Barto no longer thought like an intelligent human being. Instead, he relied only on instinct and unbearable bloodlust. He rushed in without forethought, without care, without any sense of self-preservation. After all ... he had a spear.

The boar tried to feint, to react, but Barto gave the Enemy no chance. He swung again with the staff, drawing a bright red line of blood and putting out one of the beast's eyes. Crimson and yellow body fluids oozed through smashed skin on the boar's snout. It leapt forward, driven by insanity and pain.

Now, Barto used the spear with finesse.

A great calm flowed through him, as if the rest of the world had slowed down, and he saw exactly what to do, exactly where to hold the spear. The sharpened point neatly plunged through the ribcage of the beast and skewered its lungs and heart. Showering a wet-iron smell in the air, the creature lay quivering, trembling ... dying.

When Barto came back to his senses, he saw that his legs had been slashed open by the boar's tusks. The deep gouges left him bleeding, but oddly without any sense of pain or injury. He looked down and studied the corpse of his opponent, the Enemy. Now he had killed. Barto had fresh blood on his hands, real blood from a vanquished opponent.

He liked the sensation.

He knew that this had been no simple exercise. He knew the boar could well have killed him, and that other trainees who had vanished from the barracks must have failed this part of their instruction.

But Barto had succeeded. He was a killer now, and he was one step closer to becoming a soldier.

3

Time didn't matter. For a soldier, time never mattered. He awoke hours, or days, later back in the HQ infirmary and repair shop—patched up, drugged, but fully aware. A hairless chimpanzee tended him, leaning over in a cloud of disinfectant scents and bad breath. The chimp medical techs knew how to bandage and fix battlefield wounds. They could do no surgery that required finesse, but the soldiers required nothing that needed delicacy for cosmetic effect.

Once injured, if a soldier could be fixed, he would be sent back to the battlefield. If his wounds caused the chimp medtechs too much trouble, he would be eliminated. Every surviving member of the squad bore his share of scars, burns, scabs, and callouses. No one paid attention to these trophies of war; they were part of a soldier's life, not a badge of honor or bravery.

Since Barto hadn't been eliminated, he assumed he must have been fixed.

He sat up on the infirmary cot, and the hairless chim-panzees hurried over, uttering quiet reassurances, a few English words, a few soothing grunts. Triggered by his awak-ening, a signal was automatically sent back to his squad commander.

Barto listened to an assessment of his repaired leg, his stitched muscles and skin, and his bruises and contusions. Not too bad, he thought. He'd suffered worse, sometimes even in training with other soldiers (especially during the initial few months, when they'd first been given their own sets of armor).

He remembered that back then his comrade Arviq in particular had thought himself invincible....

During downtime before the soldiers crawled into their assigned sleeping bins, the other squad members were required to file through the infirmary to see their injured comrades. Some came only because of orders to do so; most of them would rather have been sleeping.

But the invisible commanders planted instructions to go to the infirmary simply so that other soldiers could see the wounded, could see what could happen to them if they weren't careful ... but also so they could see that they just might survive.

Recovering, Barto sat up in the uncomfortable infirmary bed and watched the other soldiers come in. His pain went away with another automatic rush of endorphins to deaden his unpleasant sensations ... or perhaps his own determina-tion was enough to quell the nerve-fire of agony.

The fighters filed by. He recognized few of them, all strangers without armor and helmets, though he could have identified each one by the serial numbers displayed on their fatigues. These were soldiers, cogs in a fighting machine. They didn't have time to be individuals.

When Arviq came up at the end of the line, he stood brusque, nodding gruffly. "You'll mend," he said.

"Thank you for saving me," Barto answered. It was the closest thing they'd had to a conversation in a long time.

"It's my duty. I await the day when you can fight with us again." He marched out, and the others followed him. Barto lay back and attempted to sleep, to regain his strength. Through sheer force of will, he growled at his cells and tissues to work harder, to knit the injuries and restore him to full health....

Day after day, lying in the infirmary and waiting proved far more difficult than any combat situation Barto had ever encountered. Finally, after a maddening week of intensive recuperation, directed therapy aided by medical technology and powerful drugs, he was released from his hospital prison and sent back to the front.

Where he belonged.

4

———

The battlefield screamed with pain and destruction, explosions, fire, and death—but to Barto, after being so long in the sheltered quiet of the infirmary, the tumult was a shout of exuberance. He was glad to be here.

The soldiers raced across the ground, each in his own squad position, weapons drawn. They had already driven back the Enemy, and now the fire of laser-lances grew even thicker around them as the others became desperate. They pressed ahead, deeper into enemy territory than they had ever gone before.

Their helmet locators for sonic mines and shrapnel grenades buzzed constantly, but the reptilian part of Barto's brain reacted without volition, hardwired into fighting and killing. He dodged and weaved, keeping himself alive.

His point-man, Arviq, jogged close beside him, and Barto extended his peripheral vision behind the dark visor to enfold his comrade into an invisible protective sphere. He would assist his partner if he got into trouble—not out of any sense of payback or obligation, but because it was an automatic response, his own assignment. He would have done the same for any other soldier, any member of his squad—anyone but the Enemy.

Precision-guided mortars scribed parabolas through the air and exploded close to any concentration of soldiers who did not display the proper transponders. Amidst screams and thunder, a massive triple detonation wiped out over half of Barto's squad, but the others did not fall back, did not even pause. They drove onward, continued the push. The fallen comrades would be taken care of somehow, though no one knew how the bloodhounds would ever make it this deep into Enemy-held territory.

This far behind the main battle lines, the Enemy numbers themselves were dwindling, and Barto fired and fired again. The laser-lance thrummed in his gauntleted hands, skewering a distant man's chest plate and leaving a smoking hole.

But it wasn't really a man, after all. It was the Enemy.

The chase continued, and the survivors of Barto's squad ran in the direction of what must have been Enemy HQ. In his dry, dusty mouth he could taste the sweet honey of victory.

But suddenly, unexpectedly, they triggered a row of booby traps that did not appear on their helmet sensors. Camouflaged catapults popped up, spraying near-invisible clouds of netting, monofilament webs as insubstantial as smoke but sharper than the most deadly razor.

The flying webwork engulfed four soldiers near him, and they fell into neatly butchered pieces. But oddly enough, so did three of the Enemy men rushing in retreat, as if they themselves hadn't known of these defenses. But their own visor sensors must have been keyed to booby traps they themselves had planted....

Though the questions astonished him, Barto did not pause. His job was not to analyze. Paraplegic computer tacticians and the invisible battlefield commanders did all that work. The voices in his helmet told him to push forward, and so he pushed forward.

Arviq ran beside him, still firing his laser-lance—and numbly Barto realized that most of the other soldiers were dead. His squad had been decimated ... but the Enemy was nearly eradicated as well.

War often required sacrifices, and many soldiers died. But a victory would pay the bloody cost ten times over. They had never gone so far.

The thrill of seeing the Enemy nearly exterminated gave Barto all the enthusiasm he needed, even without an adrenaline rush augmented by injectors in his armor. With a shared glance behind opaque visors, he and Arviq both had the same thought, and ran forward with their four remaining companions. They couldn't stop now.

Then large gun emplacements popped out of the ground, more massive than anything he had ever seen before. Barto reeled in unaccustomed confusion—the Enemy had never exhibited technology like this! Automated fire rained down on them, super powerful laser-lances far more devastating than any of the handheld rifles.

Soldiers screamed. The blasts were like belts of incinerating flame, vaporizing armor and leaving not even bones for the bloodhounds to retrieve. The firepower pummeled anyone who came close, whether friend or Enemy. They had no chance, no chance at all.

An explosion ripped out a deep crater ten meters from them. Someone screamed, but Barto had no voice. The automated superlasers continued to track across the ground, pinpointing armor, crushing any movement. Barto watched the beams sweep closer, vaporizing everything in the vicinity. His four remaining squad members died in a puff of blood-smoke and molten armor plate.

On impulse he grabbed Arviq and shoved him hard toward the fresh crater. Together, the two dove into the raw trench just as the splash of disintegration passed over them. The voices in his helmet turned to a rainstorm of incomprehensible static.

Within moments the battle stopped. Everyone else was dead.

All of the laser fire and explosions ceased. All the Enemy, all of the squad, every living thing had been annihilated.

Without saying a word, Arviq hauled himself to his hands and knees and reached over to shake Barto, who also recovered his balance. The two of them sat panting for a moment, stunned but still determined. Neither of them—in fact, no one they knew—had ever been so far behind Enemy lines.

They rose up slowly and carefully into the crackling silence, afraid of other targeted automated systems. Clods of dry dirt fell from their armor. Dust and crackling ash roiled through the air … but nothing else moved.

"We won?" Barto asked. "Is the war over?"

"I hope not." Arviq turned to him, his mouth a grim line beneath the opaque visor of the helmet. "The war will never be over. But we may have won this battle."

Barto raised his helmet over the rim of the blasted crater. No weapons responded to the motion. The battlefield remained eerily quiet with only the faint sound of coughing fires and settling dust.

"Must be the Enemy encampment," Arviq said with a grunt. "Increased defenses—maybe even HQ." He grinned. "Success!"

But Barto wasn't so sure. Moving with tense caution, he climbed away from the crater. "No, not HQ. The defenses killed as many of them as us. ID transponders were useless."

Arviq joined him, sole survivors on the sprawling battle-field. Barto could see where the huge gun emplacements had raised up. Adjusting his visor filters, he spotted different infrared signatures, metallic traces, solid structures and hollow passages beneath the scarred ground.

Amazed, Barto crept forward. "We've discovered some-thing. We're required to investigate."

"No, back to HQ," Arviq said. "We must report. Our squad was wiped out."

But Barto shook him off. He stood determined, looking ahead across the scabbed landscape. "Not until we have hard reconnaissance. This could be important."

Arviq hesitated only a moment. Neither outranked the other, and they had no time for argument, but the other soldier quickly came to his own decision. "Yes. Reconnais-sance is part of our mission."

Most of the time, sly intelligent cats would creep through the darkness, observing Enemy strongholds and reporting back to HQ. But the squad had gone farther into Enemy terri-tory than any known advance, and they might have new infor-mation. That was the most important thing. They weren't doing it for the glory or for a possible promotion, or for any sort of reward. Barto and Arviq would take the risk because it was their duty.

"My head, my thoughts ... are empty," Arviq said, tapping his helmet.

Barto adjusted his earphones, but still received no transmission and no commands. An uneasy silence echoed in his head. The speakers growled no more repetitive commands to attack and kill.

"How can you stand it?" Arviq looked at him.

Barto took a deep breath. "No choice. Tolerate it."

Crouched low, they trudged toward the automated gun emplacements, but the motion sensors did not reactivate. The weapons had gone through their program and wiped out the threat. Somehow, the two comrades had slipped through the cracks. They could move forward.

Barto and Arviq found a metal hatchplate in the half-hidden superstructure of the enormous laser-lances. Barto sat down and pressed his helmet against the hatch, carefully listening for any vibration, fully tense. Any moment now he expected the destructive fire to rain out again.

He tugged on the hatch, looking for access controls. "We can infiltrate," he said. "It's an underground bunker. Maybe weapons storage. We can bring supplies or power packs back to HQ."

Together they wiped off dust and blasted dirt from the plate, used tools at their armor belts to crack open the seals, and finally they lifted the heavy hatch.

Still no voices came to their heads, no instructions. The two soldiers were on their own. Barto didn't like it one bit.

They dropped down into the opening, where a steel ladder led into a maw of shadows. They descended, gripping rung after rung with gauntleted hands. If this was Enemy HQ, Barto thought, it was a much larger complex than anything he and his squad had ever lived in.

Finally, the ladder ended in an underground tunnel with the hatch cover high above them. Barto paused for a moment to scan the surroundings, then they walked forward into dim silence. The tunnels seemed empty, barely used, abandoned for a long time. Barto realized the Enemy soldiers could not have emerged from this place. No one had walked down these access tunnels in a long, long time.

As point man, Arviq led the way. He strode forward, hands on his weapons, ready for anything. A soldier had to be flexible and determined. The small tunnel lights gave little illumination, but their helmet visors augmented the ambient photons.

Cameras in their helmets recorded everything as reconnaissance files to be downloaded back in HQ. They continued for what seemed like miles, trudging deeper and deeper into the earth. This place was an important facility, possibly a central complex ... but Barto couldn't begin to understand it.

From up ahead came a faint throbbing from generators and heavy machinery. Finally, they saw brighter light, thick windows, rectangular plates that shone through to another world, a subterranean complex that seemed like a mythical land. Inside huge grottoes, pale ethereal people moved about wearing bright colors. Plants of a shockingly lush green, garish hues that Barto had never seen before, drew the two of them forward like magnets.

"What is this?" Arviq asked. "Some kind of trick?"

"Paradise."

As the soldiers approached, unable to believe what they

were seeing, they crossed an unseen threshold, a booby trap. They heard a brief hum, a crackle of power surge. Barto reacted just in time to feel a sinking despair—but not fast enough to get out of the way.

A pressing white light engulfed both of them, swallowing them up. In an instant, Barto's visor turned black, then so did his eyes.

5

When he awoke, the assault on his senses nearly knocked him back into protective unconsciousness. Sounds, smells, colors bombarded him like weapons fire. His armor and helmet had been stripped away, leaving him vulnerable; without it, he felt helpless, soft-skinned, like a worm.

The bed beneath him was warm and soft, disorienting. A gentle and cozy light surrounded him instead of the familiar garish white to which he was accustomed back in his own barracks. Each breath of the humid air was perfumed with a sweet, flowery scent that nauseated him.

Was this an infirmary? Barto turned his head gently, and a raging pain clamored inside his skull. The place reminded him oddly of the time he had been helpless and healing from his previous injury ... but he saw no hairless chimpanzees, no robotic medical attendants. The sheets were soft and slick, vastly different from the other rough, sterile coverings.

Grogginess smothered his mind and body. Barto tried to

return to full awareness ... but something was wrong. His body remained sluggish and unresponsive, as if the accustomed chemical stimulants were not being released according to program. He needed adrenalin; he needed endorphins.

Arviq lay on another bed beside him, similarly prone, similarly stripped of his armor. When Barto turned his head and directed his gaze in the opposite direction, he was astonished to find another person by his shoulder. Not one of the enhanced animals bred to attend the regiment ... but a woman, a lovely creature with short, honey-brown hair and a shimmering purple garment so brilliant and dazzling that it made his eyes ache.

Responding with combat readiness, he sat up with a lurch —but the woman rushed over and shushed him with a gentle touch. "Quiet now. Everything's all right. You are safe here." Her voice sounded like sweet syrup. Alien.

Arviq stirred beside him, groaning in confusion and growing rage.

Then Barto remembered a legend, a story told on the field during the quiet times between battles when some soldiers were more frightened than others. It was a hopeful myth of what happened to brave and dedicated fighters after a death in battle. Was this ... Valhalla?

He glanced over at Arviq, his face contorted with confusion. His eyes glimmered with dark fires. "Are we dead?"

The woman laughed like tinkling crystal. "No, soldier. We are people like yourselves, human beings."

She didn't look like him, though, or any other person he had ever seen. Barto shook his head, refusing to acknowledge the pain left over inside. He'd had enough experience with pain. "You're not ... soldiers."

The woman smiled and leaned closer to him. A warmth radiated from her scrubbed and lotioned skin. He had never noticed a person's physical features before, never paid attention ... and he'd never seen anything so beautiful in his life.

"Everyone is a soldier," he said, "either for our side, or the Enemy."

The woman continued to give him a slightly superior smile. "You are soldiers, my friends ... but we are not. Not here." She gave a gesture to indicate her entire underground world. "After all, it's a war. You're fighting and dying." Her thin, dark eyebrows rose up in graceful arches on her forehead. "Did it never occur to you to ask exactly what you're fighting ... for?"

With a sudden burst of energy and an outcry of rage, Arviq lunged up from his bed, reaching out with clawlike hands, his face full of fury. Even without armor or weapons, any soldier knew how to kill with his bare hands. Somehow he found the energy to lash out, to propel himself into a combat frame of mind.

The woman staggered back from the infirmary beds, startled. Barto saw shadows, more people moving behind observation windows, automatic devices activating. There was another flash of white light, and again he lost consciousness.

6

When Barto awoke once more, he was alone in a room, clad in soft pajamas with more slick sheets wrapped around him. He found his bed too pliant, too yielding, as if it meant to be comfortable with a vengeance.

The gentle sound of running water trickled from speakers embedded in the wall. The white noise had a soothing effect, the opposite of the perpetual, pressuring commands that had droned into his ears from helmet speakers. Now, the image of a soporific, bubbling brook made him want to lie motionless in a stupor.

He no longer even seemed alive.

This room was smaller, the walls painted pastel colors instead of clean white. The illumination was muted and warm, like sunlight through amber. It made his head fuzzy.

Stiffly, Barto rolled over and found that Arviq wasn't with him this time. His comrade had been taken elsewhere. Was this some sort of insidious Enemy plan? Divide and conquer, separate the squad members.

Had he fallen into some new kind of warfare that went beyond violence and destruction to this personality-destroying brainwashing technique? Barto snarled and tried to find a way to escape—a captured soldier's duty was to escape at all costs.

He didn't hear a door open, felt no movement of the air —but suddenly the beautiful woman stood there with him, setting a platter down on a ledge formed out of the substance of the wall. She leaned over his bed, her entire body smelling of gentle flowers and perfumes. She smiled down at him, parting soft lips to reveal even white teeth. Barto started, ready to fight with hand-to-hand techniques even without his armor or his weapons—but she made no threatening move.

"My name is Juliette," she said, then waited as if he was supposed to recognize some significance to the name.

He answered as he had been drilled. "Barto. Corporal. E21TFDN." He rolled off the serial number in a singsong chant, "Eetoowun teeyeff deeyenn." He had spoken it more than any other word in his lifetime. Then he formed his mouth into a grim line. That was all he had been trained to say. The Enemy rarely, if ever, took prisoners. Everyone died on the battlefield.

"I brought food for you ... Barto." Juliette picked up a steaming, spicy-smelling bowl from the tray on the ledge. It contained some kind of broth laced with vegetables, even a little meat.

Though he could withstand long periods of fasting, Barto realized how hungry he was. He'd been trained to shut off the hunger pangs and nerve twinges in his digestive system. But he also knew to take nourishment whenever possible, to maintain his strength.

She extended a spoon, and Barto raised his head to accept a mouthful. The spoon was metal with rounded edges. Even such a crude and innocuous weapon could be used in many different ways as a killing instrument. He could have snatched it from her—but he did not, taking the mouthful instead.

The flavors exploded around his tongue, and Barto nearly choked. It was too intense, too spiced, too fresh—experiences his mouth had never had. Back in the barracks all soldiers ate a common meal, a protein-rich gruel that served as sustenance and nothing else. He'd never before dined on a preparation in which someone had cared about its flavors. He didn't find it at all pleasant.

Juliette gave him another mouthful, and he forced himself to eat it. But he did not let down his guard for an instant.

"The stun-field should have no residual effect on you, Barto," she said. "You'll regain your strength in no time." Her voice sounded odd in his ears, pitched with a higher timbre, musical rather than the implacable instructions that had poured into his ears from the helmet's speakers.

"I'm strong enough," Barto said. "Where is my comrade?"

"He's safe and being tended—but we thought it best to separate you." She took the bowl away, then stood back to appraise him. "I'm curious about you, Barto, Corporal, E21TFDN. I want to be your friend—so let's just use our first names, all right?" She brushed her hand along his arm, and he recoiled at her touch; it felt like warm feathers tickling across the skin. "Can you stand up? I'd like to take you for a walk to show you where you are."

Barto did not argue with her. Regardless of her intentions,

Juliette's offer would allow him to continue his reconnaissance. She could show him whatever she wished, and he would gather information. Without the helmet visor and its implanted cameras, he would have to observe with his own eyes, and remember details. But it could be done.

As he swung off the bed, the loose-fitting pajamas felt strange on him, not hard enough, not safe. He walked on the balls of his bare feet, every muscle tense, searching for mysterious threats as Juliette led him out of the room. She took him down underground corridors into even richer light. They passed beautiful images of scenery, forgotten forests and lost mountains ... waterfalls and lakes unlike anything he had ever seen on the battle-scarred combat fields.

"Who are you people?" Barto said. "What is this place?"

"We're civilians. We went underground centuries ago to escape the fighting, while our armies defended us against the invasion."

Barto tried to assess the information, to fit it like puzzle pieces into the sparse information in his mind. "My squad is ... part of the defenders? We fight against the invaders?"

She looked at him with a curious, placid expression. Her pale skin, delicate bone structure, and pointed chin gave her an ethereal, elfin appearance. "No one knows which side is which anymore."

Other people, similarly pale-skinned and soft-looking, observed the pair as they walked by. Some smiled, some drew back in fear. Many regarded him with cold, fish-like interest. Juliette seemed to enjoy the attention she received just by being with him.

Barto scanned his surroundings for a way to escape and return to his squad. But then he remembered that, except for

Arviq, all of his comrades were dead, annihilated by the immense gun emplacements that protected this underground shelter. Back at his own HQ, the databases must have already recorded him and his point man as casualties of war.

Juliette talked as they continued, her voice a pleasant mélange of words. She told him of their days of peace and shelter down below, how the survivors had made an entire world down here by excavating tunnel after tunnel. There, the civilians did what she called "the great work of humanity"—composing music, dabbling in art, writing poetry and literature ... though, if they remained isolated down here without experiencing the hard edge of life, Barto didn't know how they found any material to incorporate into their creations.

Though she turned at intersections, descended to different levels, walked in circles, Barto never lost his bearings. He imprinted a map of everything they encountered, knowing he might need to use it later. On his own.

Juliette took him to a greenhouse where the smells nearly stifled him: humid air, the odors of vegetation and mulch, flowers bursting forth like explosions from mortar fire. Pollinating insects flitted from blossom to blossom, and brilliantly ripe vegetables and fruits made his eyes hurt.

He heard the drip of irrigation systems, saw colorful birds hopping from plant to plant, and a shiver went up his spine. Everything was so quiet here, so gentle. It made him feel too full of energy, too restless.

Barto remembered when he'd been forced to recuperate in the HQ infirmary as the hairless chimpanzees tended to him. He had been bored and frustrated ... but with a goal—to heal, so he could go back and fight. He had managed to wait until his body returned to its optimal condition, when he could go out and serve his purpose in life.

Here, though, these people had a quiet calmness about them, an air of superiority ... with nothing else to do. Juliette seemed to enjoy it, seemed proud of being a civilian.

Barto had never experienced such vibrant beauty, the smells, the music

... the sense of peace. His body rebelled at the thought, but as the hours went by in the beautiful woman's company he began to feel his resistance crumbling. This was all new to him.

As she showed him their underground "paradise," Barto followed her and listened. Finally, in exasperation, he turned to Juliette and asked, "So there's no war here?" He couldn't believe it. Such a concept had never occurred to him. "No battles?"

"Oh, we have a little." Juliette smiled, then gestured him forward. "Here, let me show you. Maybe you'll find it comforting."

She led him down smooth passages where the temperature grew cooler, the smell more metallic. They walked down glass-walled hallways until they reached a control center.

Battle plans. Tactical maps. Troop movement displays.

"This is how we maintain our edge, Barto, and our window on the outside world." Juliette's people sat at stations in front of the shifting screens, their fingers raised across control panels. Terrain grids spread out in front of them in bristling colors.

High-resolution panels showed other soldiers, people in familiar armor and helmets, jittery point-of-view images transmitted from visor cameras. Civilian men and women leaned over, punching in commands and speaking into microphones.

"Move left. Open fire."

Another man with a deep voice droned, "Kill the Enemy. Kill the Enemy. Kill the Enemy." He sounded bored. The others looked very relaxed in their positions.

Barto stared with shock as he realized that these were the voices he'd heard in his helmet all his life: directing him, helping him plan his attack. These were his ultimate commanders in the war.

Astonished, Barto looked over to see Arviq also standing inside the control room, chaperoned by a civilian man, also dressed in a loose jumpsuit. His point man's chaperone demonstrated the workings of the controls. Arviq's eyes were wide as he watched the battle.

Sensing the new arrivals, Arviq looked up to see Barto. Their eyes met, and hot understanding flashed between them. This was the ultimate headquarters of their army. Arviq reeled from the revelation, but Barto felt a nagging question in the back of his mind. He wondered if other civilians in this control room might be directing the Enemy troops in a similar fashion.

Safe in their protected bunkers, these isolated civilians played the deadly war like a game, an exercise. They'd lived here for so long, so comfortably, they seemed uninterested in winning the conflict or ending the crisis ... merely in maintaining what they already had.

"So you see, Barto," Juliette said, touching his arm again—this time he did not withdraw so quickly—"we understand what you go through. We're familiar with the war, we're there with you inside your head during even the most terrible missions. We know how difficult it is for the soldiers." She smiled. "That's why I'm very glad to offer you asylum here. Stay with us." Now she sounded coy. "I'd be ... very interested in getting to know you better."

Arviq glowered, out of his element. The chaperone next to him nodded toward Juliette, and she said, "You see, Gunnar is also taking good care of your comrade. Stay here. Consider it well-deserved R&R."

Barto looked around, saw the controllers, heard the familiar command voices. He answered gruffly, "I'm a soldier. I follow orders." Even if it meant he must stop fighting for a while.

7

―――――

Once the two prisoners had resigned themselves to their situation, they were allowed to speak with each other, though neither Barto nor Arviq had ever had much use for conversation. For a week they had made no violent gestures and learned to "behave themselves"—as Juliette described it. As a reward, Barto and Arviq were allowed to sit next to each other in the dining hall.

The room was a large chamber with plush seats and long tables. Lights sparkled from prisms overhead, and the air was redolent with the rich smells of exotic dishes. Various salads and broiled fishes and interesting soups were spread before them. The hall echoed with a murmur of voices.

In his training sessions, Barto learned about the horrors of being a POW, should such a fate ever befall him. But he was now confused, not sure which orders to follow, what was the proper course of action. Juliette had insisted he was their honored guest, not a prisoner. Should he still try to escape? These civilians had given him food and shelter, and a soft bed, though he desperately wanted his narrow basket-bunk back. He longed for the decisive voice in his ears that commanded him to do his duty—but Barto no longer knew exactly what his duty was.

Arviq looked at his plate and poked at the gaudy, frilly dishes that had been served to him. Other soft-skinned civilians walked by, staring at them, whispering to each other. One reached out to touch Arviq on the shoulder, as if on a dare; the soldier lashed out like a python, and the two observers scampered away giggling, as if titillated by the thrill they'd just received.

Barto felt as if he and his point man were on display, specimens for a zoo … or humiliated members of a captured Enemy force, dragged before the public as trophies. Shrouded in silence, Arviq seemed to be doing a slow burn as he sat staring at his food, glaring at the other people.

Barto tried to calm himself. His own emotions seemed so much flatter since he'd been brought underground, his mind dulled—as if the adrenaline pump, endorphin enhancers, even his root survival instincts had been neutralized. Listening to the muted drone of conversation and music around them, he thought back longingly to the cacophony in the mess hall at his old barracks.

He remembered the clatter of metal trays, the crash of armor plates as soldiers jostled each other. With wordless camaraderie, the squad members sat on hard benches, grabbed their utensils, and gobbled their tasteless food. Together, they recharged their batteries and stoked the fires that they would need for combat in their next mission.

While none of the soldiers knew each other very well, each knew his place in life, his purpose … and his Enemy.

These underground civilians had nothing to compare with that.

Juliette sauntered up to them, her elfin features positively glowing, as if Barto's presence had increased her own standing among her people. She walked with her tall friend, Gunnar, who had spent days escorting Arviq. She looked down at the food on Barto's plate and clucked in a mock scolding tone that he should eat more.

Barto felt a strange sensation in his stomach and heart, as if he were basking in the sunlight of her presence. How could Juliette make him feel proud that she had chosen him for her special attentions? He had never been singled out for anything before.

On the days when Juliette brought him to the breakfast hall, Barto was glad to see her, eager to hear her voice, just to look upon her face. As his senses had become accustomed to his environment, his tongue relished the taste of fresh fruits and breads. The flower scents in the air smelled sweet, and he didn't flinch when Juliette touched him this time, taking him by the elbow. He liked the softness of her fingertips, the way they moved up and down his arm. He felt that he wanted to be even closer to her, to allow her into the walled fortress of himself.

"Do you like it with us here?" Juliette said with a hopeful, even plaintive, lilt to her voice. Ignoring Arviq, she touched the lumpy intaglio of scars on his forearm, tracing patterns and imagining his terrible wounds, as if she had never seen such marks before. "I'd like for you to stay with us, Barto ... with me." She reached across the table to clasp his hand, and he felt the urge to withdraw. What was she doing?

Gunnar's narrow face seemed drawn and concerned. He

shook his head gravely. "You know how he's been trained. You know what this man has been through. He's not a toy for you, Juliette."

"I know exactly what he is," she answered. They both talked as if Barto wasn't even there. "And that doesn't change my wishes one bit."

With intent, flicking eyes, Barto followed the conversation, the conflict. If Juliette wanted him to stay here—and he vehemently wished that she did—then he would stay.

He'd seen the control chambers, the computer screens. He knew that these were the ultimate commanders of the war, the people who issued the instructions through his helmet speakers. His job had been to defend these civilians, to protect them ... and if Juliette should happen to give him leave to stop the fighting and stay here, with her, then he would follow orders.

Moving around behind him at the dining table, Juliette held out a large purple flower, its petals like a soft starburst. With particular care, she slid it into the close-cropped dark hair behind his right ear. Then she clapped at her audacity and at the spectacle she had made. He flushed.

Barto did not remove the flower, knowing it was somehow special to Juliette. The other civilians in the dining hall spoke to each other, pleased and entertained. Then Juliette danced away with tall Gunnar beside her, leaving the two soldiers to continue eating under the scrutiny of the curious observers.

Arviq looked across the table at him, scowling at his comrade's behavior. He narrowed his flinty eyes at the flower in Barto's hair. "You look like a fool," he growled, and snatched it away.

8

Back in his too-peaceful quarters with the door sealed and locked from the outside, he lay on his too-comfortable bed and then finally curled up on the hard floor. He would sleep better that way....

He dreamed of other times, when there hadn't been so much peace, when he had felt alive and useful and necessary. Where he had known his place in the world.

After one particularly furious foray, he, Arviq, and five other squad members crept ahead, continuing to approach the blasted Enemy territory even after the main conflict was over. They followed trails of blood and footprints, drag marks left by the bloodhounds that had come to retrieve the bodies of Enemy soldiers.

In the dream Barto increased his visor's sensitivity to search for infrared traces of organic waste or warm blood droplets. The enhanced bloodhounds were not trained to cover their trails, and with their heavy, mangled burdens, they left a path that was easy to follow, even across the blistered landscape.

The squad followed the trail back to a shielded Enemy encampment. Barto and his comrades prided themselves in their bravery (or foolhardiness), and they charged into the bunkers with their weapons drawn, their adrenaline packs tuned to full output. Their laser-lances blasted the hinges off the doors and made short work of the plasrock bricks that shored up the damaged buildings.

Within moments, Barto's squad had breached the outer defenses and came in firing. No mercy. Many Enemy soldiers were still in their armor, but their weapons were locked in recharging racks. Others fought hand-to-hand, never giving up.

Barto's team suffered heavy losses, but during the fight he was dizzy with exhilaration. By himself, he vanquished fifteen of the Enemy soldiers; altogether, his squad destroyed the entire outpost. Total victory.

Throughout the combat exercise, during the screams and explosions, the violence and death, Barto had felt a sure camaraderie between his fellow soldiers. He never let doubt enter his mind, never a question. He knew exactly what he was doing here.

The Enemy bloodhounds, locked in their small home-kennels, bayed until Arviq cut them all down. The dogs seemed to know they had been responsible for betraying their masters' location.

With a resounding cheer of triumph, the survivors of Barto's team gave a shout to celebrate the defeat of the Enemy. Then, as part of a ritual for such infrequent but absolute victories, the men reached down to tear the helmets off the Enemy corpses, taking them for souvenirs.

Barto removed the helmet from the soldier he had just killed, then looked down to see the visage of the Enemy.

In his dream, the face belonged to Juliette.

9

As days of contained rage and frustration built within him, Arviq found that he didn't even need the supplemental adrenaline pump from his dismantled armor. This was all wrong! His blood boiled, his anger rose into a thunderstorm of fury—and he unleashed it upon the walls, the bed, anything in his room. His cell.

Arviq didn't want to be a prisoner of war. He wanted to fight, to kill the Enemy. He had been bred and trained for nothing else.

The quiet stillness of this underground civilian world, the soft fabrics, the perfumes, and the too-tasteful food ... all pushed him into a frenzy. He tore the coverings off his bed and thrashed about, ripping the sheets to shreds. He howled and screamed without words, a bestial cry of damnation. He pounded on the door, but it only rattled in its grooves. Then he threw himself upon the bedframe itself, yanking and pulling, until finally he uprooted it from the walls.

He didn't know if anyone was watching him, nor did he care.

Arviq hurled himself against the metal wall, battering his shoulders, bruising his muscles, but feeling no pain. His body was accustomed to running on the ragged edge of energy, and he had been resting here for days, storing up power in his muscles. Now he released it all in his frenzy.

His attack made marks on the wall, left some smears of his own blood. His fists caused dents. The sealed door rattled again in its tracks; it seemed looser now. He pounded and pounded, receiving no answer.

Finally, Arviq returned to the ruined bedframe, wrenching free a strip of metal that he could use as a crowbar. He had to escape. He had to get back. He didn't belong here.

He wedged the ragged end of torn metal into the door track and pushed, prying ... bending. The door began to buckle, and Arviq worked even harder.

10

____

After his nightmares had left him like exorcised demons, Barto fell into a deep slumber and awoke incredibly refreshed. Sometime in the middle of the night he had crawled back into his bed and rested peacefully.

A soldier had to be flexible, had to adapt to new circumstances. At last, he had begun to do just that.

When Gunnar and Juliette came to fetch him, he sensed their tension. The other civilians continued to stare at him, as they had done for days, but now they held a greater glint of fear in their eyes, a more uncertain look on their faces. Barto couldn't understand it, because for the first time since he'd come to this place of sanctuary, he felt more relaxed, more at ease, as if his life had indeed changed.

Seeing how the underground people had changed, how their attitude toward him had shifted, Barto knew something must have occurred. He could sense it. "What has happened?" he said.

Gunnar looked at him and answered crisply, "Your friend

Arviq has gone on a rampage. He broke out of his room, and he's escaped."

Barto bolted to his feet. He understood Arviq's impulses. He had felt them himself, and now alarm bells rang out in his head. "What has he done?"

Juliette took a deep breath and blinked her deep brown eyes, as if the subject itself made her uncomfortable. "He broke his way out of the room. He smashed some windows in the corridors, destroyed one of our greenhouses. That was an hour or so ago. No one has seen him since."

Barto pushed his half-finished breakfast away and stood tall and strong. Called back to active duty. He didn't need any more sustenance, no more food to distract him. His mind became focused again, delving into the old hunter/survival mentality.

"I know how he thinks, and I know what he's doing," Barto said. "You cannot let him get away."

"We can't stop him," Gunnar said. "He'd kill all of us if we tried."

Barto shook his head. "You don't understand what Arviq can do, or what will happen if he gets away from this place. You can't just ignore him." Then he looked over at Juliette again. He finally admitted to himself that she was beautiful.

"Can you stop him?" Juliette said. "It would be to protect us."

"I will need my armor and my helmet if I'm going to do this right."

11

At first the armor felt rough and strange, but rapidly Barto adopted it as a second skin. The protective covering belonged, as much a part of him as his bones and muscles.

Looking at her soldier, Juliette wore a concerned expression, as if he had too easily stepped over the brink. Barto saw something unreadable deep within her brown eyes, a flush on her elfin face, as he picked up the helmet. He looked at her uncertainly one last time, then seated it firmly on his head. He pressed the side speakers against his ears, lowering the visor in place so that he looked at her through filters and scanning devices instead of his own eyes.

Barto drew a deep breath, stretching his chest against the breastplate armor plate. He flexed his arms against the hard bicep plates, the forearm protections, the gauntlets. His torso was solid and impenetrable. His legs and back, shoulders, hips, everything could withstand the worst that Arviq threw against him.

Barto was invincible.

"I must stop him before he leaves," he said. "He'll report the location of this place to HQ."

Juliette hesitated, moved forward and then stopped, as if she wanted to embrace him but was afraid to. Barto was glad she didn't. He didn't want to get close to her, like this.

The tall chaperone, Gunnar, stood beside her, his face grim, and he drew her back. "Let him go now, Juliette. He has a mission."

Barto turned and marched out of the room, summoning up his mental map of the underground civilian sanctuary. He would begin in Arviq's quarters, where the point man had smashed his own room and broken loose. It would not be too difficult to pick up his former comrade's trail. Barto knew how to track down a quarry.

Leaving the other inhabitants behind, he followed the tunnels. Most of the civilians reacted with fear when they saw him now. They hid within their own quarters or clustered together in the communal halls, though only one unarmed soldier had gone on a rampage. It was all beyond their experience.

All of these people cowered down here, helpless. And Barto was the only one who could protect them.

Though Arviq had not been able to retrieve his armor or his weapons, Barto did not underestimate him. A properly trained soldier could fashion defensive materials out of just about anything.

At the pried-open door, he stood motionless, assessing Arviq's damaged room, saw how his comrade had wrenched open the barricade using a piece of the bedframe as a lever, how he had battered the walls with his bare hands. Barto saw blood but knew that Arviq would pay no attention to such minor cuts and bruises. Not Arviq.

Barto had seen him through much worse.

One time on a reconnaissance and destruction mission, Barto and his point man had ventured into the crumbling ruins of what must have been an impossibly large building, now scarred, empty, and blasted. The structure had fallen into rubble with haphazard girders and broken glass protruding from poured stone walls.

They had chased several Enemies into the wreckage. Their senses screamed that it was probably an ambush, but still the two soldiers had followed, weapons drawn, confident that they could defeat their opponents. He and Arviq separated and traveled along different passageways, using their scanners to pick up infrared footprint traces.

Barto had proceeded cautiously, but Arviq, incensed and determined, charged through the darkened halls, knocking wreckage aside. Finally, he had crashed down a rickety iron staircase that shattered into rust as he stepped on it. And he dropped through to the underlevels....

When Barto had found him later, he saw that Arviq had broken his left leg in two places and had sprained his right ankle. His helmet visor was cracked and damaged—yet still Arviq had pulled himself along to find the Enemy. He certainly had.

Though severely injured and at an extreme disadvantage, Arviq had slaughtered both of the Enemy soldiers....

From their missions together, Barto knew that his comrade was utterly relentless, feeling no pain and no fatigue. Nothing would stop him from escaping the underground enclave. He would never give up.

And neither would Barto give up. He was the only thing that could keep this civilian paradise protected and intact.

He strode out and moved briskly along the corridors. His bootsteps ricocheted off the metal walls. Arviq had smashed windows and thrown loose objects from side to side, leaving a painfully clear trail—until he had learned better and sensibly stopped his rampage.

Then tracking him became more of a challenge. Barto called up a detailed implanted map of all the underground corridors, which Juliette had added to the information systems in his helmet.

Arviq was running blind, by instinct, just trying to escape, but his movements displayed a pattern. On the map gleaming inside his visor, Barto could see the best paths, learn where to go ... where to intercede.

Arviq didn't have a chance against a fully armed, fully outfitted soldier, like Barto.

He marched along, his senses tuned to a high pitch. He moved carefully in case the other soldier had set up some kind of booby trap or ambush. That was to be expected. Arviq must know Barto would come after him.

Because the other soldier was without his armor, his bare feet left a trail of infrared images on the clean floorplates. The marks were old and fading, but still identifiable with Arviq's genetic signature: droplets of sweat, skin particles, even stride length gave evidence of his passage. The other man was still bleeding from one of the cuts he'd inflicted upon himself in escaping from the room; occasionally a telltale crimson droplet reinforced Barto's tracking.

The control voice returned, insistent and self-confident. It comforted Barto, who had lived his conscious life hearing the words: "KILL THE ENEMY! KILL THE ENEMY! KILL THE ENEMY!" He no longer felt so alone.

According to the map display, Arviq had made it to within several hundred meters of the long access ladder that led up a shaft to the outside—the battleground where their squad had been killed.

But Barto also knew he had cornered his quarry.

At an intersection of the dimly lit corridors, a framework of girders and support beams held up the ceiling. The place had been long-abandoned by the underground civilians.

Barto's visor-sensors detected a large smear of blood at floor level in a corner, as if Arviq had rested there ... or as if he had encountered an Enemy, and they had struggled, hand-to-hand. The blood was fresh, wet, warm in IR—like a sign emblazoned there to draw his attention.

Too late, he realized the ambush. From the shadowed support girders above, Arviq let out a loud cry and dropped on top of him. Though he had no armor and no weapons, the other soldier crashed down upon him with brute force. Barto might have found the conflict absurd if Arviq hadn't been so determined, so passionate—if the other man hadn't been his own comrade for so long.

Arviq wrapped his left arm in a vice-lock around Barto's neck, trying to wrench the helmet off his head. With his other hand he tried to grab one of the ID-locked weapons sealed in armored holsters on Barto's hips.

Barto rose up like a tank, as if his armor gave him stimulus and energy, though Juliette had told him his artificial adrenaline pumps were disconnected from the suit.

Inside his ears, the helmet commanders shouted, "KILL THE ENEMY! KILL THE ENEMY! DON'T LET HIM

ESCAPE!" With a weird disorientation, Barto thought the voice sounded like Gunnar's.

Without letting go, Arviq fought like a wild thing, clamping his knees on either side of Barto's armored chest, trying to tear the helmet off. When Barto staggered backward, slamming his comrade against the metal wall, Arviq let out an explosive exhale of pain and surprise. Barto recovered his balance and slammed him against the wall a second time.

Arviq struggled but would not let go. He continued pounding with naked fists against the impenetrable armor.

"Come with me!" Arviq shouted loudly enough to penetrate the heavy ear coverings, to break through the harsh command voice. "Let's go back to HQ. Back to our lives, Barto! We don't belong here."

Barto bent over and butted him against the wall, hearing ribs crack this time. Arviq's grip finally loosened. He wheezed in pain, coughed blood. "Let me go then. Just let me run from here. I'll leave." Arviq slumped to one side and scrambled to his feet. Blood from his raw wounds smeared Barto's scuffed armor.

"Can't let you do that," Barto answered. "You must stay here. The commanders gave their orders. Defy them, and you're a traitor."

Arviq stood up, glaring at him. His face was uncovered, his emotions unmasked. "This isn't what we were made for. We are soldiers. War is our life. Not this ... where we're pets on display." Barto had never really studied his comrade's face before. "What happens when they get bored with us?"

Barto pressed his gloved palm against the hilt of his ID-coded blaster weapon. The device detected its proper owner and released its grip in the holster. Barto yanked the weapon free, held it in his hand.

Not far down the corridor, he could see the tarnished rungs that rose up the dark shaft. It would take so little for Arviq to scramble up the ladder, pop the heavy hatch—and be out, all alone on the blasted battlefield. Without armor or weapons, he didn't have much chance of survival—but Arviq seemed desperate enough to take that option.

Arviq gathered himself up, glared at his former comrade and stepped away. "I know what I am, and what to do." With the back of his hand, he wiped a smear of blood from his mouth. "Which one of us is the traitor, truly?" He turned and, moving slowly, not threateningly, took a step toward the ladder, the escape.

Barto raised the weapon. "Halt."

Arviq turned to look at him with flinty, determined eyes. "I'm dead down here anyway. If I can't get back onto the battle-field, then you may as well blast me now."

Barto powered up his weapon.

The other soldier took two more steps down the corridor.

Inside the helmet, Gunnar's voice shouted, "KILL THE ENEMY! DON'T LET HIM ESCAPE. YOU MUST PROTECT US. KILL HIM!" Barto leveled the blaster at the target.

Then he heard another voice—Juliette's—muffled and distant, but coming closer. She cried out, running down the long-abandoned corridors toward him. "Don't shoot, Barto. You must learn not to kill if you're going to stay here."

"Kill! Kill!" Gunnar's voice bellowed.

Arviq turned as Juliette appeared, all alone, her elfin face distraught. Then he used the moment of distraction to dash toward the rungs.

"KILL!" shouted the voice in Barto's ears again. And he did.

Depressing the firing stud, he blasted his former comrade in the back as he ran. Arviq had no armor, no protection whatsoever. The bolt flared out and incinerated him, turning the other man into a smoking pile of burned bones and cooked flesh that fell in a heap on the floor, as if still trying to run.

"No!" Juliette cried out, but it sounded like a pout. Barto turned to see her standing there. Her expression was stricken, and then even more terrified as he faced her, the charged weapon still in his hand. "I wanted you to stay here with me," she said. "It's a better life, but you've got to learn not to kill. Stay away from violence. You've earned it. You could live here with me in peace and enjoy your life, escape the horrors of war."

"They're not horrors," Barto said in a flat voice. He refused to take off his helmet. He was a soldier now, fully armed, ready to fight. "It's the only thing I know." He holstered the warm blaster. "I can't stay here as a prisoner of war."

"But you're a free man among us," Juliette pleaded, refusing to come closer. She seemed as much confused as saddened. She couldn't understand why he would make this choice.

"I am still a prisoner," he said. "War holds me prisoner." He stood at attention, as if the feline spies were watching him from the shadows. "I must live by fighting, and I must die by fighting. I have no way to escape that."

He understood now that this place, despite its comforts and its new experiences, could not possibly be for him. Not for a soldier.

He didn't begrudge Juliette her civilian life, her pampered existence—and if these people were indeed the commanders in the war, if he was a soldier charged with protecting them, then he must go back and do his duty until death inevitably claimed him on the battlefield. And if he should happen to survive, then he would grow old and train other soldiers until the war was won and the Enemy completely vanquished.

There was nothing else for him to do.

Juliette watched him with despair, then a flash of anger in her brown eyes. Finally, her slender shoulders drooped in defeat. She said nothing else, just watched him with a flush in her cheeks.

Barto didn't know what he had really meant to her ... if he had merely been a trophy from the battlefield, something that increased her prestige among her people—or if she had really cared for him, in a way.

At the moment it didn't matter. It was irrelevant information.

Leaving his dead comrade behind, sad that the bloodhounds could never retrieve Arviq and take him back to where he could be buried with full military honors, Barto climbed the rungs of the ladder.

It was a long way to the surface, but when he released the hatch and climbed out under the open, bruised sky, he stared for a long moment. He breathed the burnt air, studied the roiling dust from distant explosions.

He lifted his visor to stare out across the stricken field with his own eyes, then he shut the hatch behind him, sealing Juliette and her world underground, keeping her secret safe. And then he strode off, heading in the direction of his HQ.

It would feel good to get back to the business of fighting once again.